Large Print Kis
Kistler, Mary.
A stranger at my door /

V W9-BYF-007

# A Stranger
## at My Door

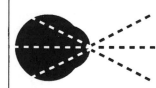

This Large Print Book carries the
Seal of Approval of N.A.V.H.

# A Stranger
## at My Door

*Mary Kistler*

**Thorndike Press • Waterville, Maine**

Published in 2001 by arrangement with Mary Kistler.

Thorndike Press Large Print Candlelight Series.

The tree indicium is a trademark of Thorndike Press.

The text of this Large Print edition is unabridged. Other aspects of the book may vary from the original edition.

Set in 16 pt. Plantin by Elena Picard.

Printed in the United States on permanent paper.

**Library of Congress Cataloging-in-Publication Data**

Kistler, Mary.
    A stranger at my door / Mary Kistler.
      p. cm.
    ISBN 0-7862-3441-5 (lg. print : hc : alk. paper)
    1. Amnesia — Fiction.  2. Traffic accident victims — — Fiction.  3. Galicia (Span : Region) — Fiction.
    4. Americans — Spain — Fiction.  5. Large type books.
    I. Title.
    PS3561.I827 S77 2001
    813'.54—dc21                      2001027779

*For Jan, who reminds me of Lisa*

# *Prologue*

The wail of the siren ceased, dying on the rainy night like an interrupted scream; and the last patrol car to reach the scene of the crash came to a jerking halt. Almost before the motor stopped, officers Newcombe and Riley were out of the car and running.

The accident area, picked out in flares and highlighted in a rosy horror of its own, was cordoned off for two hundred yards. Police crossed and recrossed the circle of light and ambulance attendants scurried through the veils of rain like anxious white mice.

As the newly arrived officers stepped inside the ring of flares, Newcombe let a strangled, "My God!" escape him, then clenched his teeth in embarrassment. He was new to the force and inclined to say things he regretted in front of that stony-faced partner of his. But even a veteran like Riley would have to admit this was one awful mess.

A black Lincoln and a red sports car had met head-on and were crushed together like paper cars. A girl's shoe lay on a glittering pile of glass. From one of the five stretchers lined up along the shoulder of the highway blood streamed in scarlet ropes.

"What happened?" Riley asked an officer who had arrived earlier.

"We figured the driver of the Lincoln must have missed the road construction signs in the rain. When the road narrowed he swerved and skidded, crossing the yellow line into the oncoming lane."

"All dead?"

"These two here on the nearest stretchers. An elderly couple, trapped in the Lincoln."

Newcombe looked at the stretchers. Both were covered, but from one of them the feet of a woman stuck out beneath the blanket. There was a peculiar flatness where the woman's face should have been and blood seeped up through the blanket from some terrible and secret wound beneath.

Newcombe shivered. No wonder, with that damned rain beating a tattoo on his helmet and running down the back of his neck.

"And the others?"

"The fellow on the end there, who looks like he might have been the driver of the sports car, seems in fair shape."

Glancing down at the end stretcher, Newcombe saw a dark-haired man sprawled under a blanket. The man's black brows were drawn together in a deep frown; he looked as though he slept, dreaming an incredibly painful dream.

"How about those two girls on the middle stretchers?"

"Badly off."

Crossing over to help another patrolman put more blankets over the stretchers, Newcombe looked down at the girls. They both had long dark hair and the lines of their bodies under the wet blankets were slender, youthful. Near in age, Newcombe thought, say early twenties, maybe. Might be from the same family.

As he threw the fresh blankets over them, he saw that the eyes of one girl were wide with shock, miniature flares reflecting back from their glassy depths. The other girl lay breathing shallowly; part of her face was crushed in and her hair was matted with rain and blood.

"Were the girls from the same car?" Newcombe asked.

"Can't tell. All of them except the middle-aged couple in the Lincoln were thrown free and the wallets and handbags lost or ground into the mud. If they all die, it's going to be something straightening out this crowd."

"One of the girls just died," Riley said.

Newcombe studied the girls more closely. Old Stone Face was right. The girl who was having all the trouble breathing wasn't breathing any more, but it took some looking to realize this. Newcombe, cold to the bone inside his wet uniform, turned away.

# Chapter 1

We crossed the runway at the Madrid airport, my silent companion and I, just as the door of our plane opened, cutting a lighted square out of the iron-dark night.

We quickened our pace, and as we reached the bottom step of the ramp, I faltered. From weariness? Perhaps. I was still shaky from my hospital stay in San Francisco; and our flight from San Francisco to Madrid had been a wearing one.

Now, boarding the plane for La Coruña, we were entering the last phase of the long journey from California to northern Spain, and this realization blew through my brain like an icy wind.

My escort reached out and caught my elbow. As he steered me upward into the glowing door of the plane, I knew that my stumbling pause had not come from weariness alone. It had been an instinctive drawing back.

Soon we would be reaching our final destination. There I would come to know the meaning of the frightening step I had taken (could it have been only twenty-four hours ago?) when I had decided in a single unreal moment, to come away with this man who insisted so fervently that he was my husband.

Perhaps he was.

When you have no memory, all men are strangers.

As we stepped inside the plane, an Iberian stewardess in a caped red uniform smiled and greeted us in Spanish. Then her eyes flicked past me to light with speculative interest on my "husband." Enrique was not unaccustomed to such glances, I was sure.

He was from Galicia, and he had the startling good looks that I learned later were not uncommon in the northern Spaniard. Dark blue eyes, bequeathed by Celtic forebears, making an arresting contrast to the black hair and pale skin. And then there was the manner, the attractive easy arrogance of the Spaniard, and always that look of having just unbuckled a sword and tossed it aside.

As we started up the aisle, I noticed other interested feminine glances aimed in Enrique's direction, and I wondered whether, in that strange and separate time before the accident (in that other life of mine that Enrique had gone to such infinite pains to explain to me) I had minded this sort of thing.

Hopefully I waited for a vestigial prick of jealousy. There was nothing, no caring of any kind. The fact that Enrique and everyone concerned with my affairs insisted that he was my husband brought no response from me but confusion.

He was as much a stranger now as he had been in that nerve-shattering moment two weeks ago when, rising from the depths of a month-long period of unconsciousness, I had opened my eyes to see an unfamiliar hospital room . . . and a man sitting beside my bed, staring at me intently.

Remembering the intensity of the stare, remembering the stillness of his closed untelling face, I moved quickly away from Enrique now, up the aisle of the plane. I wanted space between us, the chance to breathe away the panic this memory of him brought.

It was no use. He stepped easily in behind me, overtaking me and touching me lightly on the arm.

"Here we are, sixteen A and B," he said, leaning down to store the small luggage. "Give me your coat. You'd like a seat by the window, wouldn't you?"

I swung out of my coat before he could help me, before he could touch me again. "I don't mind the aisle if you prefer the window."

A harsh "No, thank you," was all I got for my trouble.

We settled in and buckled our seat belts. Enrique was frowning and a dark flush had risen in his cheeks. He hadn't missed the implication of the coat byplay, then. Such moments were becoming more frequent and more awkward, but lost in my own private nightmare, I paid little attention.

The pilot revved the motors and the plane shuddered, moving into position for take-off. Then we were streaking down the runway, lifting toward the stars.

Next stop, La Coruña. Chilled by the thought, I began the silent childlike recital that had brought me comfort in the anxiety-ridden hours following my decision to come to Spain with Enrique.

It was the right thing, the only thing to be done. Still convalescing from the accident, your memory gone, no family to turn to but an aging uncle who made no offer of asylum, you had to come away with this stranger-husband. Your doctor and the police working on the missing identification papers, assured and reassured you. No one doubted that Enrique was your husband.

A voice whispered inside my head: No one but you.

*The accident had been a terrible one, the doctor had said, a head-on collision late at night. A heavy car (a Lincoln, he thought) had swerved, gone out of control and jumped the divider, crashing into Enrique and me as we came from the opposite direction in a sports car. On Highway 101, it was, just out of San Francisco. With both cars so badly smashed, everyone thrown free except the middle-aged couple in the big car, and all identification burned or lost in the wreckage, there had been a proper muddle for a while. To add to the confusion it was discovered that one of the passengers in the Lincoln was a girl about my own age and size, whose hair was black like mine. Odd, wasn't it?*

*Very odd. And what happened to the girl?*

*Died at the scene of the accident. Inevitable, of course. One side of her face was crushed in. The other two passengers in the Lincoln, who turned out to be her mother and father, were dead on arrival.*

*And how was I identified?*

*By your husband, of course. No problem there.*

*No, no problem there. In the freaky way of ac-*

*cidents, Enrique's injuries had been relatively minor — a concussion and three broken ribs. The second he could get to his feet, he had come to my room and stayed there, never leaving me unless ordered to. He wanted to be near when I regained consciousness so that I wouldn't be frightened. A very devoted man, the doctor had said.*

Now, glancing sideways at Enrique, I thought: very devoted. And I shivered.

"Do you want your coat?"

"No, thank you."

The stewardess leaned over us, inquiring about drinks.

"A martini on the rocks for me, please. Champagne for my wife."

Wanting to assert myself, I said deliberately, "I think I prefer a martini, too, if you please."

Enrique waited until the stewardess had gone before he spoke. "You've always disliked martinis."

Had I? No way to remember, and I felt the sting of tears in my eyes, the easy tears of the convalescent. Too much of that lately, and I hoped that Enrique hadn't seen. But he had.

"You mustn't mind so much, Lisa. You'll only make matters worse."

I turned back to the window and stared

16

out into the country of the night. Like my mind, a blank landscape with nothing but shadows and starlight to guide me in my search for myself.

And I had made no progress so far. An alarming realization, one that compelled me once again to sift back through the only memories I had, all encompassed in the two short weeks since I had awakened from my unconscious state. Still, a small bright patch in the darkness.

I thought now of the warm concern of the hospital nurses, the kindness of the doctor who had tried so earnestly to reassure me, never growing restive under the barrage of questions I couldn't stop asking.

*Why this doubt about who you are? the doctor had asked. Not only has your husband identified you but your uncle, as well.*

*My uncle. One stranger backing up another, I thought coldly. When it was discovered that I had lost my memory, an elderly uncle from Los Angeles (my only family, Enrique had said) was brought to see me. My uncle and I spent a morning together, and he hadn't awakened the faintest glimmer of recognition in me.*

*That afternoon, looking searchingly into the troubled face of my doctor, I began my questions all over again.*

*A mistake could have been made. I feel I'm not the person you think I am, that I might be that other girl.*

*You've been identified. Why should you question this identification?*

*I've told you. It's a feeling, a strong feeling . . .*

*Your feelings aren't reliable evidence at present. You must go by facts. And one of the facts is that the other girl was identified by a cousin from the East Coast.*

*But the girl's face was crushed in. And the nurse told me the cousin hadn't seen this girl in five years. He could have made a mistake.*

*Your uncle has identified you, and your own husband has also. What possible reason could a stranger have to claim you for his wife?*

*I don't know. Were all the driver's licenses lost?*

*Lost or destroyed.*

*But California driver's licenses are on record somewhere, surely.*

*In Sacramento. Computerized and filed, the photos kept separately. All of this available by official request . . .*

*Could the police get this information for me? Could I see my photograph?*

*But you had no American driver's license, according to the police.*

*Wasn't that rather peculiar, a Californian of my age not driving?*

18

*No, since you seem to have lived most of your life abroad. Your husband has told you all he knows of your background, surely?*

*Oh, yes, he's told me. But I'd like to hear what he told you and the police.*

*Well, to begin, that you grew up in Madrid, but he met you here, not in Spain. In Palo Alto, about a year ago, when you were both going to Stanford graduate school. That may account for your not taking out an American license. Perhaps you lived on campus and didn't need a car. Perhaps you and your parents preferred to spend home leaves in Europe instead of in the States, so you wouldn't have had a license here earlier. There're all sorts of possibilities. You probably have a Spanish license, but no one knows about that.*

*Or cares, I thought, since I have been so readily identified by this determined and persuasive man.*

Did the other girl have a license on file?

*Not in California. She and her parents were from out of state.*

Could her license be traced?

*To what purpose? The girl's cousin identified her and took her body back to the East Coast, along with the bodies of her parents. Your husband identified you. The police are satisfied. Except in your own mind, there's been no question.*

At no point had the doctor lost patience with

19

*me, but he had put the matter plainly to me at the last. You must get over this notion that you were not identified correctly. You must begin by trusting the people around you, the people who are trying hard to help you. You have a fine husband who wants to take care of you. Trust him — trust me . . .*

And so, at last, I had come away with Enrique.

What else could I do?

I looked at my "husband" from under lowered lids. An extremely attractive man, but a wintry and austere one, a man who cast a cold shadow. Could I have married such a man?

Sharp, intuitive denial cut through my darkened mind like a blade of light, leaving me shaken, cold around the mouth.

I turned my head and looked out the window again, trying to focus on anything, the lanes of clouds, the gliding stars, but all I saw was my own reflection in the window, my own haunted face staring back at me.

# Chapter 2

"Your drink, madam."

"Thank you."

"Since we're in Spain now," Enrique said, "you will, I hope, try to speak Spanish."

I lifted my glass and took a long fiery swallow, then another and another. When I finished I sat back, enveloped in a sudden glowing warmth.

"How can I speak Spanish," I reasoned politely, and evidently too loudly, "if I don't know Spanish?"

In a low, amused voice, Enrique came back with, "Stop shouting, please."

"Who's shouting?" I asked suspiciously.

To my surprise, Enrique laughed. I realized that I'd not heard him laugh before, and I was disarmed by the change the laughter brought.

"You are. Smashed on one drink. And as for the Spanish, it might come back to you if you'd try to speak it. You used to speak it extremely well, you know. Although," he added, "you did have a slight accent."

"I might say the same for your English. Which you speak with a British accent. Which is worse."

"What was that again?" Enrique asked, his voice still edged with laughter.

Whether it was the drinks or the teasing trend of the conversation, this was the friendliest exchange we had managed. I knew the doubt hadn't gone but receded, and distrust would return. The anxiety would come back, too, igniting at every veiled remark or puzzling reference.

As though he couldn't resist the impulse, Enrique reached out and laid his hand on mine.

"Please remember again, Lisa . . ."

I jerked my hand away. The cold wind was back, freezing the laughter in my throat.

If Enrique had tried he couldn't have chosen a more devastating method of plunging me back into the shadows. Had he done this deliberately? If he were not my husband, the last thing he would want would be for me to regain my memory. What better way to keep me disturbed and off balance than to alarm me with unwelcome advances and reminders that my memory was gone?

I wanted to hit back as cruelly as I could. "Whatever I mean to you, you're still a stranger to me. So until I can remember you as my husband, would you please keep your hands to yourself?"

I watched the flush rise in Enrique's face again. There was no question that my proud Spaniard was sustaining a few blows on his own account.

This was the first affectionate overture Enrique had made for a long time now, the first since the day I had regained consciousness and found him sitting beside my bed. I had stared at him without moving. Then he had leaned over, taken me in his arms, and saying "Lisa, Lisa," had buried his face in my hair.

I had lain against this stranger, shuddering.

As the shuddering went on he'd pulled away from me, got to his feet, and stood back from the bed.

"Lisa . . ."

"I don't know you."

"I'm your husband . . ."

"Perhaps you are, but I don't remember you," I answered, my voice rising. "I don't even remember my own name, so how could I know you? All I ask is that you not touch me."

And he hadn't, not after that.

This was an unpleasant memory, and I was glad when the stewardess returned, bringing our supper trays. I began to eat, then gave up and drank my coffee in silence.

Enrique had eaten in silence, too, and when he finished he said, "If you have forgotten your Spanish, you will have to relearn it. You will find little English spoken in our village."

Had I ever spoken Spanish? Had I ever lived in Spain?

A fierce, familiar longing consumed me. I was burning up in my desire to know one single truth about myself. There was no one to give me information but Enrique, and no way to know whether he dealt in lies.

Once again I reviewed the facts of my past, as (presumably) I had related them to Enrique before the accident.

I was an only child and had spent part of my childhood in Madrid, where my father headed up an American oil company. Returning to the States for college, I attended Stanford. During my senior year, my parents, en route to California to visit me, were killed in an air crash.

I stayed on in Palo Alto, taking my Masters. In my final semester I met Enrique, who had come from Spain for special courses at Stanford Business School. We fell in love, and when Enrique's scheduled year was up we were married quietly in Palo Alto. We were heading for a week's honeymoon in San Francisco, before going to Galicia to live, when we crashed, six weeks ago, on our wedding night.

The telling of it didn't take long. Bare bones, with no thoughts or feelings to add, to remember.

And were these facts true?

*What possible reason, the doctor had asked, could a man have for saddling himself with a convalescing wife who had no memory, unless this wife were his own?*

But my rebellious heart questioned still . . . for some reason not to be guessed at.

I had no proof of Enrique's duplicity. I only knew that on the dark plain where I now lived, my intuition was constantly setting off alarm bells regarding him. Still, there had been no choice but to come away with him; and until I could discover the reason for this alarm, or until my memory came back to guide me, there was nothing I could do but wait.

I glanced at Enrique. No question that my earlier rebuff had offended him.

"We'll be coming into La Coruña soon," he said stiffly. "You'd better fasten your seat belt."

I obeyed, looking down through the starlit darkness as the plane descended. Lights winked at me through drifting clouds, from a country I had never known, or was unable to remember.

Swamped in loneliness I turned back to Enrique, wanting to re-establish contact. I needed someone and I had no one but him.

"Tell me about your house again," I said, broaching the one subject I knew he couldn't resist.

The thaw set in immediately. Any mention of his home or Galicia could effect this change in him.

"The house is just as I have described it to you. Made of stone. Beautiful and old. It has stood for a century, alone on a high cliff by the sea."

Enrique's voice warmed with each word, but, to me, the prospect was daunting. When I recalled what he'd told me of his family, my enthusiasm diminished further. A large family, with several of his relatives permanently in residence.

"A house of that size. And all those people. How shall I manage? I can't imagine myself being in charge of such an establishment."

"No one will expect you to be in charge of anything. My grandmother, with a staff of servants, has always seen to the running of the house. You're only to enjoy yourself and get well. There's a month of summer left. Time for you to grow brown and healthy again."

It seemed a strange, purposeless life. "Won't there be anything for me to do?"

"I can't think of anything just offhand."

He smiled at me, a brilliant, disarming smile. "Unless you count the signing of some papers. That ought to use up at least five minutes of your time. Then we'll think of something else to occupy you."

Enrique's too-casual reference to the signing of papers riveted my attention. I sat caught in stillness. For the first time my doubt and confusion were replaced by a diamond-clear emotion.

Fear.

Here at last was a fact to back up instinct, a reason why Enrique might be determined to bring a stranger away with him. He needed a wife to sign papers. Had I been brought to Spain as a surrogate wife, substituting for the girl who had been killed in the crash?

Surely there was a discrepancy here. My signature could not possibly match up with that of the other Lisa, that other, very dead Lisa.

There was no way that Enrique could bring off such a thing. This my mind told me; but my heart began to pound with a heavy, painful beat.

"I'm afraid my signature would be of little use to you," I said in an embarrassingly unsteady voice. "I'm not even sure I can write any more." (This much, at least, was true.)

"No difficulty there," Enrique answered easily. "Because of your memory loss your signature may look quite different. But as long as you sign in front of witnesses who identify you as my wife, and who attest to the fact that the document was signed in their presence, all's well."

The pounding had reached my head now.

How frighteningly legal it sounded. And how naive of me to think that my "husband" could have overlooked a matter of such importance. I was learning fast about Enrique. A daring man, but one who covered his bets; and if I were not the real Lisa, he had covered this one very neatly, indeed.

The signing was to take place in Spain, in a remote Galician village before witnesses of Enrique's own choosing. Señor Enrique

Fuente's wife, carefully identified, signing a document at the request of her husband.

Who was to question? To know? To care?

"I won't sign any papers," I said.

"Of course you will," Enrique answered pleasantly. "And they must be signed immediately, upon arrival."

# Chapter 3

From Madrid to La Coruña we had flown even with the morning star, through clear black night. But now, approaching the airport, we descended into smoking mist.

We deplaned, to find a damp wind in our faces and the smell of the sea on the wind.

Enrique pointed to a blanket of lights below us. "La Coruña, off to the right, there. The airport, as you see, was built high above the city, on a plateau."

I heard the excitement in his voice, and I glanced in the direction of the lights. I said nothing.

Once inside the airport, Enrique found a seat for me. "Sit for a minute while I have a look around for Alfredo. I wrote him to meet us, but I don't see him. Some sort of mix-up, I suppose."

I didn't know who Alfredo was, and I didn't care. I had more alarming matters on my mind, and when Enrique walked away from me, I sat staring after him, desperately frightened.

The matter of the signing of the papers was a chilling new dimension in my relationship with my "husband," and the urgency accompanying the request more chilling still. Enrique had mentioned the papers before we had so much as put down in La Coruña, and had added that they were to be signed "immediately, upon arrival."

*Your memory may return piecemeal or it may come back abruptly and completely, Dr. Markam had said. An incident, a crisis, anything may trigger the return. Your past could be restored to you in an instant.*

Enrique, who had always listened so intently to anything concerning my amnesia, would not have forgotten this. Not Enrique. Was he moving with such speed and determination because he was afraid that at any moment I might remember who I was?

Had I been that other Lisa, surely such haste would not have been necessary. The real Lisa would have signed papers for her husband at any time. Another point. Enrique had apparently anticipated resistance from me. His out-of-the-blue approach, the disarming smile before the casual request, the pressing urgency, all indicated this.

I felt a rush of wind from an open door, and pulled my coat more closely about me, but I found no comfort. A chill of the spirit, then, not of the body, cold that came from the wintry breath of my own fear.

All of my ambivalence about my "husband" was gone at last. I recognized that I had made a terrifying mistake in coming away with this man.

A flickering behind my eyes told me that one of those tiresome headaches that had plagued me since the accident, was beginning. I pressed my fingers to my temples.

One thing was clear to me. I did not dare remain in this threatening situation. I must get to a safe place to wait out the return of memory.

Where was I to go?

It was humiliating to realize that I had no choice. San Francisco was the only place I could remember. I would have to return there.

Once arrived, it would be necessary for me to contact Dr. Markam again, and perhaps Evelyn Wells, the nurse who had been so kind to me in the hospital, and try to enlist their support in making a new start. To turn up defeated and still lost, still asking for help, would be added humiliation; but I must not think of that.

It would not be easy to inform Enrique that I had changed my mind, that I had decided to leave Spain. And I would have to borrow the return fare. Humiliating (again) to have to ask such a favor. How would I pay the money back? Somehow. In installments if necessary.

Tomorrow, after a proper night's sleep, when I had myself more in hand, I would tell Enrique that I was going back to California.

This decision was the only unequivocal one that I had made since my illness, and this new certainty brought peace. More exhausted than I had known, I leaned my head against the back of my chair, and fell into a sudden light sleep. I may have slept for several minutes, but it seemed only an instant before I felt a finger flick my cheek.

"Last lap of the journey, my love," Enrique said.

How dared he use a term of endearment to me, pretending that the mention of the papers meant nothing, resuming his role of devoted husband as though the matter had never come up?

But Enrique's sleight of hand personality, his ability to present a new image of himself or reverse an old one in an instant, appeared to be one of his greatest assets. It's all done with mirrors, I thought bitterly, as I got to my feet.

"I couldn't find Alfredo, but I managed a Rent-a-Car."

Picking up my overnight bag, Enrique guided me out into the mist-strewn night. He had found a parking place near the airport entrance and had already loaded our larger bags. I sank into the front seat of the car, and we were on our way.

Rain began to fall as we left La Coruña, and the road was narrow and twisting. I could see nothing but what was caught in the sweep of the headlights: a crumbling stone bridge, grapevines polished with rain, ferns spread like green lace fans over the lower slopes of a mountain. I could hear wind singing in the tops of trees, and once there was the liquid laughter of a mountain stream.

Enrique drove in silence. I saw weariness in his face, but there was excitement there, too. How glad he seemed to be home, and I wondered enviously what it must be like to know when you were home.

I drowsed, rousing myself only once to ask, "Did any of your family visit you in Palo Alto? Has any one of them met me?"

"No. My grandmother gave up traveling

years ago. She is nearly eighty. And none of the others came to the States while I was there. You'll be meeting everyone for the first time tomorrow."

I did not reply, and after a long time, Enrique said, "We'll be turning onto our land soon."

Interested now, I sat up and looked about me as we swung off the highway onto a narrow road. Difficult to see, but I knew that the face of the land had changed, because the smell of the sea was stronger here. On one side of the road pines flashed past, but on the other side there was the feel of open country.

Enrique explained, "There's a *ria* on our left, a sunken valley where the sea encroaches at high tide. We have these marshes all through Galicia. You'll soon see the house at the head of one of the *rias,* on a hill."

I shivered. I was listening to the wind and thinking of the rain slanting down on the marshes, and of a dark house on a hill.

We had begun to climb and the trees, now on both sides of the road again, were thick, ancient, and sparkling with rain in the car's headlights. We made another turn and I heard gravel beneath the tires.

I huddled into my coat. The tone of the

wind had deepened and somewhere a night bird screamed in the valley. We burst out of the trees, swung around a sweeping curve of drive, and stopped.

"Home," Enrique said.

I stared at the house, appalled. It was a heavy and forbidding place, wrapped in rain and lighted by two lamps, one on either side of a great carved door. I couldn't guess at the size of the house but it seemed to stretch away from the door in tremendous wings. It was of honey-colored stone, darkened with age; and its roof slanted down into wide overhangs. The thin windows, recessed and now filled with darkness, were like slits in a medieval fortress.

Enrique got out of the car and came around to open my door. Picking up my overnight case, he helped me out, and we ran up the steps, pressed the bell, and waited.

Enrique swore softly. "Where is everyone? There should be a maid to let us in . . ."

As though on cue the door swung open into a lighted entrance hall and the maid stepped aside for us to pass. There was no question that she had been asleep on the job because her frilly cap sat askew on her shining hair, and her face, perspiring from her dash to the front door, looked like a damp apple blossom.

*"Buenas noches, señores,"* and then with a slight gasp, *"bienvenido!"*

In spite of his obvious irritation at being kept waiting, Enrique laughed at this attempt to rally.

*"Buenas noches,"* he replied and then he said to me in English, "They've run a new one in on me."

*"Cómo se llama, por favor?"* he asked, speaking again to the maid.

*"Feli, señor."*

I guessed he was asking her name. It was a pretty name. Everything about the servant girl was pretty, and the sight of her comforted me.

*"La señora está muy cansada, Feli. Puede arreglar todas las cosas para ella?"*

*"Sí sí, sí, señor,"* Feli answered, grabbing up my case and steering me anxiously toward the stairs.

"I'm going back for the rest of the luggage," Enrique said as I passed him. "Can you manage with the one bag?"

"Yes."

"Feli will see you into bed then and find anything you need. Good night, Lisa."

"Good night," I answered, and I went blindly up the curving staircase, Feli guiding me firmly.

At the top of the stairs we came out into a

marble-floored gallery, with closed doors on three sides. Feli turned me in at the first door, and I crossed the room and sank down on the bed.

The room was large, with high ceilings and a beautiful oriental rug on the floor; this much I took in while Feli helped me undress. As I fell in between elaborately monogrammed sheets, ironed to a chilly crispness, I told myself that it was a good thing I wasn't staying long. I'd freeze to death in this place.

Then, on the edge of sleep, I remembered my manners. "Thank you, Feli."

"You're welcome, señora," she answered in English.

My eyes flew wide open. "Do you speak English, then?"

"Only a little bit. But I understand *más* — more."

Well, thank God for that, I thought, and we smiled at each other. I closed my eyes, exultant because I felt I had found a friend. Then I wondered uneasily why this fact seemed so important to me.

The answer came through waves of sleep: Because you must stop off for a night or two in this house of strangers, and in this dark and lonely place you need a friend.

# Chapter 4

I slept deeply that night and awakened refreshed. Enrique's house, I thought. I was
cheered because I remembered this. It was a
moment of conscious recovery, and I reveled
in it.

But my peace was short-lived.

Turning my head and looking curiously
across my room to open french doors where
sunlight blazed on a glassed-in balcony, I
saw a pair of long legs encased in work
pants, stretched out from a wicker chair.

Enrique.

I swung out of bed, my cheeks burning,
and fled to the bath. I hated the way Enrique
assumed proprietary rights over the rooms I
slept in. He had been constantly about in
my hospital room; and there had been that
awkward afternoon in Madrid, when we
shared a hotel room, resting between flights,
dozing fitfully on our separate twin beds. I'd
liked none of it.

But all that would soon be over. I would leave tomorrow if reservations were available. Then Enrique could come and go in whatever rooms he chose, since I would no longer be "in residence." Having come to this pleasant conclusion, I looked about me.

My bath had blue tiled walls, a bathtub that stood waist high on curved legs, and a washbasin that looked big enough to drown in. Organdy curtains blew out from my open window and towels warmed on heating racks. My toilet articles had been laid out. I crossed the marble floor and began my chilly ablutions.

After I'd washed up, I brushed my hair, and twisting it into a loose knot on top of my head, I turned to find my robe hanging on the back of the door. I pulled it on. It was quilted silk, lemon-colored, and as soft as smoke. I was sure it had cost the earth, as the other clothes that Enrique had bought for me must have done.

Taking such things from a man I planned to part company with shortly was unpleasant. Still, there was no other choice.

Our trunks had been sent ahead of us, before the wedding, Enrique had said; but the luggage and clothes we were traveling with were destroyed in the accident and had to be replaced.

As I came out of the bath and crossed the room to the balcony, Enrique got to his feet. He stood in a pool of scattered newspapers, relaxed, appearing more approachable than I had seen him; and this was all to the good, considering what I had to say to him.

"Good morning, Lisa. I've rung for your breakfast."

"Thank you." Then, feeling oddly contrary, I added, "I'm not awfully hungry, I'm afraid."

Without comment, Enrique drew out a chair for me, and then he said, "Honest-to-goodness Spanish sunlight, courtesy of Galicia."

"Lovely," I answered carelessly, but it was lovely.

And I liked the balcony. It was a long one that ran the length of the east side of the bedroom and was entirely enclosed by sliding windows. There were white wicker chairs with faded red cushions; a scattering of wicker tables; and geraniums in wooden tubs, flaming in the corners of the balcony.

Looking down on the dark plumes of trees tossing in the wind, and seeing a seagull riding the air currents high above the *ria,* I guessed that the wind blew hard here even on the brightest days.

I settled into a chair as Feli arrived with

my breakfast tray. Her cap was aslant again and her face becomingly flushed in her anxiety to please. We smiled and greeted each other. Feli settled the tray on a small table in front of me, and arranging everything with care, departed.

Enrique retreated behind his paper. I was relieved, after what I had said about not being hungry, because one look at the food made me ravenous. I started in, polishing off a slice of melon, two crusty, warm rolls lavishly spread with unsalted butter, crisp bacon, and two cups of coffee with hot milk.

Evidently Enrique hadn't been as absorbed in his reading as I had thought, because he said in an amused voice, "Shall I ring for your lunch and dinner now?"

"*Touché,*" I answered ruefully, as he lowered his paper.

"Not to worry. I'll beef up the staff and put the cook on overtime."

His eyes, narrowed with laughter, had turned as blue as a mountain lake. We were experiencing, for the second time, a rare, uncomplicated moment of friendliness.

It did not last long. Enrique, it seemed, could not leave me in peace. Or did not wish to.

He got lazily to his feet, strolled over to my chair, and stood looking down at me.

"No feeling of *déjà vu* now that you're home?"

Desolation swept me. For a time I had forgotten my amnesia; but how skillfully Enrique always managed to remind me of it. I turned my face away toward the bright valley, but the day seemed to have lost its light.

"No. And Spain is not my home."

"Not Galicia, since you told me once that you'd never been this far north."

"I wonder if I told you that?" I asked coldly.

"Of course, you told me. How else would I know?"

How, indeed?

He reached out and lifted a strand of hair that had worked loose from the knot on my head and had fallen against my cheek. His hand brushed my skin, and my body froze under his touch.

He remained by me for a moment longer, then moved abruptly away to the windows. With his hands plunged into his pockets he stood looking out at the wheeling birds, his shoulders rigid.

We were back at our battle stations.

"My family will be in from church shortly. Will you please get dressed and come down as soon as possible? They are extremely anxious to meet my 'bride.' I use the word advisedly, of course."

"Of course," I answered tauntingly.

I thought back again over what Enrique had told me about his family. His parents were dead but there was a grandmother and an uncle and the widowed wife of a cousin; and a child, a niece, who was the daughter of Enrique's only brother, Pablo. Pablo and his wife were on a three-year assignment to El Aaiún, in the Sahara, where Pablo was chief engineer for a large phosphate plant. Nita had been left with her uncle and the grandmother to begin her formal schooling.

Enrique was speaking again. "And I hope you'll be at least a little conciliatory toward my family. It's important for all of us that you and they should get on together."

Enrique said this in the arrogant voice that always put my hackles up, but I was glad because I found my rising anger bracing. It made what I had to say to him easier.

"Certainly I'll be down. And I'm always pleasant to people I meet. Whether I get on with your family on a permanent basis, however, is not important."

There was a strange little pause. "Why not?"

"Because I'm going back to San Francisco tomorrow, if this can be arranged."

"Are you really?"

His body was still, but he turned his head and looked at me; his eyes, filled with sunlight, had a blind look. "So you regret coming away with me. You don't think I'm your husband do you?"

I shivered in the hot sunlight.

"No."

"And when you get back to San Francisco, how will you manage to live?"

"I'll go back to the hospital and ask my new friends there to help me get a start . . ."

"Oh, yes, the very attentive Dr. Markam."

"And the nurses. They'll help me find something to do."

"When you can remember nothing about yourself except what I've told you? Could you give me a list of your qualifications? What is your Social Security number?" he finished cruelly.

"I'd be allowed a new one. I'll manage . . ."

"You're incapable of managing. And until you are well, until your memory is restored, you will remain here."

I felt as though the breath had been knocked out of me. I hadn't expected Enrique to be pleased with my decision . . . after all, he'd had an excellent reason for bringing me here . . . but it had never occurred to me that even he would dare to try to force me into staying.

"But there's no way to know when my memory will return," I protested, totally incredulous.

"Nevertheless, you will remain here until it does."

I sat in a stunned silence until anger again rescued me. "There's no way you can keep me here against my will."

"Of course I can keep you here against your will."

"What kind of a family do you have that they would condone such a thing?"

"A family who is determined to see that you come to no harm. I have explained to them that because of your amnesia you are subject to fugues and are not capable of watching out for your own welfare. They understand that you must be accompanied by a member of the family, or one of our servants at all times, until you recover. Naturally everyone is willing to co-operate."

"Naturally."

The word seemed to come from a great distance. That was because I was back on my dark, icy plain . . . where Enrique wanted me.

*A fugue, Dr. Markam had explained, is a sec-*

*ondary lapse of memory inside the framework of a person's amnesia, in which this person actually takes physical flight, forgetting even that which he has previously remembered, awakening in another place without knowing how he got there, unable to recall what has happened during the lapse.*

Enrique, in his infallible way, had zeroed in on the one excuse for keeping me here that would seem acceptable to everyone.

"House arrest?" I asked in a voice filled with hate.

Still half turned in my direction, he sent me a glinting look. "Call it what you like."

Then he left me.

My thoughts flew like hot sparks as I dressed, dressed urgently, hounded by the prospect of Enrique's returning for me if I delayed too long.

Sitting at my dressing table, I told myself that it was ridiculous to imagine that Enrique could actually keep me prisoner here; but as I began applying lipstick I saw a dewy line of perspiration break out across my upper lip.

My "husband" had a way of doing what he set out to do.

I paused, resting a shaking hand on the table top. Why not just sign the papers, and go free? Because, a warning voice said inside me, you have no guarantee that Enrique would let you go, even then. Once you sign the papers you are expendable.

Neurotic nonsense. But the line of perspiration I had wiped away appeared again in the next instant. I knew I dared not sign the papers, not at any time, not under any circumstances.

And I would get away from this house somehow.

It would not be easy, and it would not be tomorrow. Even if I weren't being watched, there were so many things I must know, first.

How far was it to the village, and how was I to get there? Enrique had said that little English was spoken there. A small place, then. Even so, there must be a bus that passed through, one that could start me on my way toward Madrid, where I could get to the American Embassy.

I couldn't be watched every minute, could I?

Glancing into the mirror again, I was disturbed to see my cheeks flaming like poppies. I was turning feverish with anxiety and this premature planning.

I sat quietly for a bit, calming myself. I was getting nowhere with this hopeless speculation, and that flickering behind the eyes that preceded a headache was starting again. Unwise to add that problem to the stresses already at hand. I needed all my strength and wits to cope with Enrique and the meeting with his family.

I went to the closet, pulled out the first dress I came to and stepped into it. It was an off-white affair, long-sleeved, high-necked, pencil-slim.

As I passed the mirror again on my way out, I allowed myself a critical glance. The outfit came off well; I looked thin and expensive, ready for the next skirmish.

I crossed the gallery and paused at the head of the stairs. Enrique was waiting for me at the bottom. He had changed his clothes and he seemed very Spanish now. He wore a dark suit and a white shirt and his gold cuff links caught the dim light of the hallway. He looked magnificent, but I could scarcely bear the sight of him.

# Chapter 5

I came down the stairs, and Enrique and I crossed the hall in silence. From somewhere came the slow, sad tolling of a bell, a sound in keeping with the heaviness of spirit that had returned to me at sight of my "husband," a husband who, by his own admission, was also my jailer.

As we reached what I thought must be the sitting room, a door flew open and a small girl with fly-away black braids hurled herself at Enrique. He leaned down and scooped her up in his arms.

*"Tio Enrique, te amo!"*

"English, please. This is your Aunt Lisa, who doesn't yet speak Spanish. Lisa, this is Juanita, favorite niece, aged six."

Juanita twisted around in Enrique's arms.

"Is this your new wife?" she asked in a clipped British accent which amused but did not surprise me. I knew from Enrique that most privileged Spanish children had

English nannys when very young, and that Juanita's nanny had only recently departed.

What a taking little creature Juanita was, wild and merry looking. She sent me a mischievous smile which I returned, feeling better for this exchange.

"She's a pretty one, that aunt."

"She'll do," Enrique answered coldly, and then in a warmer voice he added, "Nita, I would appreciate it if you would unhand me. This is the third time this morning I've been greeted by you, and I've been nearly strangled each time."

Nita planted her satin cheek against Enrique's. "*Tio,* I'm glad you're home."

"Be that as it may, I'm tired of being choked, so let go."

Nita let go. As her uncle set her on the floor again, she said, "*Tio* Enrique, you're such a jolly man."

"Not a jolly man. A very frightening man. Ask your Aunt Lisa."

Enrique again, reminding me that he was terrifyingly aware of me at all times.

I was glad to be distracted by Nita, who took me by the hand and led me through the open doorway. Enrique followed, just behind me, taunting me with his closeness. Always there, like an icy wind at my back.

As we entered the drawing room, Nita

pulled away and went ahead. The room was so large that at first I missed the group of people gathered around the fireplace at the farthest end.

Or perhaps I missed them because the light was concentrated where I stood, light from the thin windows I had seen last night. I swung around to these windows and the sunlit outside world, but familiar fingers pressed my elbow.

"You're keeping my grandmother waiting."

We started down the room, across polished floors where Persian rugs threw deep pools of color, under high ceilings crossed with massive dark beams, past paneled walls where the gold frames of portraits caught the sun.

Feeling absurdly panic-stricken, I asked, "Does everyone in your family speak English?"

"Yes."

As we neared the fireplace area, I saw four people seated in crimson velvet chairs that flanked the fire. Two men got to their feet, but it was the grandmother I was most aware of.

Small and weightless looking, she wore a black silk dress, and a black lace mantilla covered her sculptured silver hair. Her eyes were of the same blueness as Enrique's, but they lacked the depth and clarity. Were they always so remote? She sat elegant and still, watching me come to her. Her one piece of jewelry, a magnificent emerald ring, burned from the shadows.

Enrique introduced us and I crossed to her chair. She reached up, pulled my face down, and kissed my forehead.

"Welcome to your new home, my dear."

The tone belied the words; there was no warmth of welcome here.

Did she always deal with strangers in this way, retreating behind a wall of beautiful frozen manners? Or had she taken a special dislike to me? Did she resent me because I was an American?

Shaken, I straightened up, and when Enrique touched my elbow again, I passed on to a girl about my own age.

"My cousin Antonia," Enrique said.

As he spoke, Antonia rose from one of the scarlet couches.

"How do you do?" she asked. We shook hands, estimating each other.

I thought her beautiful. She had auburn hair that fell in wings, framing a cameolike face . . . pale skin, delicate features, thickly lashed eyes. She wore a gold-colored suede suit, so soft it moved like silk against her body.

Antonia. This would be the young widow of Enrique's cousin. Enrique had had little to say about her when he'd spoken of his family, and I wondered at his silence.

I smiled at her, but I saw I would fare no better here than with the grandmother. Her eyes sparkled with hostility under the sweep of her lashes.

"My Uncle Carlos," Enrique said, steering me toward a large florid man. Uncle Carlos bowed over my hand, terminating the performance with just the slightest lingering pressure.

"Welcome, Lisa. We have, of course, been looking forward to having you with us." He took me in in one expert glance. "Yes, indeed, it's a great pleasure."

Such cordiality should have been welcome to me after the gamut of cool receptions I had run. Instead, I found myself mentally recoiling. No sight-seeing tours down dark halls with Uncle Carlos.

Last, I was introduced to a Father Fernando who was evidently there as a luncheon guest. Tall and esthetic in his black robes, he looked like a medieval saint. His features were sharply defined, honed down to the point where his bones seemed to shine through his skin.

"How do you do, Father?"

He smiled shyly and inclined his head. "Welcome to Galicia, Señora Fuente."

I smiled back, feeling a little lift of the heart. A possible friend? Someone to turn to for help?

Enrique found a chair for me. A maid brought sherry in a crystal decanter, and poured wine into glasses already filled with firelight. I was just settled when Nita appeared at my elbow, dragging an outrageous doll that was almost as large as she was.

"This is Anna, *Tia* Lisa."

Anna had a scar down one cheek, one eye was missing, and her yarn hair dangled, madly awry.

"She's beautiful," I said.

"Yes, she is," Nita agreed and there was a ripple of fond laughter.

Routine inquiries about my journey followed, while I was carefully watched from under politely lowered lids. The simplest answers became an effort for me, and it seemed to me that I could feel tension licking about my chair like lightning.

When luncheon was announced I suppressed a nervous yawn and stumbled to my feet. On top of everything else, the jet lag had set in.

The grandmother, leaning on the arm of Father Fernando, led the way out of the room. Uncle Carlos pressed forward and offered me his arm; Enrique, Antonia, and Nita followed, laughing and talking intimately together.

We left the drawing room through a door near the fireplace and came out on a landing I hadn't seen before.

This landing must be at the back of the house, I thought, at the end of the hallway that began at the front door and ran the depth of the main floor, separating the two principal wings of the house. A stairway led down from the landing and I saw that we would be descending to the next floor to reach the dining room. The kitchen and servants' quarters must be on this lower floor as well. Once again, I realized what an imposing place this was, three full floors and all of the rooms on a massive scale.

We crossed the landing under a glittering chandelier and went down a black wrought-iron stairway.

When we reached the dining room, I saw that two walls were cut by more of the thin windows, and the dark paneling was repeated here. But the extra windows made this a cheerful place. The room was awash with light, light that set the silver on the long table glinting, that raced up the bright chains of the brass chandelier, that beat across the polished parquet floors until they shone like mirrors.

I watched the ceremonious seating of the grandmother at the end of the table. Enrique then settled at its head, with me on his right. No question of the new bride usurping the grandmother's position. I was being treated as a guest. Splendid. A guest whose stay might be unexpectedly short.

Nita, propped up on velvet pillows, was placed next to me, with Anna leaning drunkenly between us. Uncle Carlos sat across from us and Antonia next to him.

The interminable meal began, wore on. I pretended to eat. The only bright moments in the whole ghastly ordeal were supplied by Nita who seemed to consider me her responsibility. There was no question that I needed a mentor, but I hadn't realized how badly, until Nita said rather severely, "*Tia* Lisa, that strand of Anna's hair is in your *gazpacho* again."

Again? Startled, I straightened Anna up, and was diverted by the action into a temporary revival.

I was glad for this because Father Fernando began to question me politely. He spoke of the coming of the Spanish to California, of the great Spanish land grants. To my surprise I found I remembered some

57

California history, and I felt excited at discovering this.

We talked together until I realized that all other conversation had ceased and everyone was listening to me with an alarming intentness. Confused by my alarm, warned by it, I ceased speaking almost in mid-sentence. Still upset without knowing why, I locked my teeth together to smother another jarring yawn. Enrique got to his feet and moved behind my chair.

"Give it up, Lisa. The next thing we know, you'll be plunging face down in the *paella*."

Even if it hadn't been 6:00 a.m. in Palo Alto and the sun blazing on the back of my neck in Galicia, I couldn't have been gladder to escape these people and this room. I got to my feet, apologizing, as the men rose.

The grandmother said, "No, please, we are the ones who should apologize. You look so well that we had forgotten your illness."

So that's the way it's to be, I thought. I was to be constantly reminded of my memory loss.

I felt color burning into my cheeks. "I am very well today, just drowsy from the time change . . ."

Then Antonia, who had spoken little during the meal, said softly, "But you have been very ill, haven't you?"

I pretended I hadn't heard, and Nita bridged the awkward moment by saying, "It's hard to eat when you're sleepy."

I was sure she spoke from experience and giving in to impulse, I leaned down and kissed the top of her shining head.

She took this salute in stride.

"Have a good nap, *Tia* Lisa," she said comfortably.

Enrique and I left then, climbing the stairs to the main floor, traversing the long hall in silence. When we reached the front entrance we paused at the foot of the central stairway. Enrique, his eyes gleaming with malicious amusement asked, "Shall I see you into bed?"

"I believe I can manage," I replied coldly, and seared by his burning glance I fled up the stairs.

I awakened sometime late in the night.

There was no light in the room but starlight, and a warm wind, filled with the scent of the sea, moved in from the balcony.

I got to my feet and padded across the floor, following the path of the wind. When I reached the balcony I found that the glass windows were sliding ones, and someone had opened them.

I settled down in the darkness, moving

with care. The balcony windows next to mine were open, too. Enrique's balcony, and I had no wish to let him know that I was awake.

I sat on, considering my meeting with Enrique's family, dreaming of escape.

After a time I heard a light rap at Enrique's door, his chair scraping back, his voice saying, "Come in. Ah, Antonia . . ."

"I saw your light as I was passing . . ."

"Splendid. Take the big chair and get comfortable. I've been hoping for a proper visit with you today, but there seemed no chance for us to be alone."

Antonia's answer was caustic.

"Are you quite certain that you wish to be alone with me, now?"

"Don't be tiresome, *querida*. Tell me how you've been keeping in the months since I've been away."

"Not months. A full year. Three hundred and sixty-five lonely days. Give or take a few."

"For God's sake, Antonia. . . . Must you?"

Enrique sounded every inch the goaded lover, half-angry, torn.

I sat motionless in my chair, my mind alight with what I was discovering. No wonder Antonia had met me brimming with hostility this afternoon, that Enrique had avoided mention of Antonia.

"I don't like her."

"Lisa? It scarcely followed that you would."

"In fact, I hate her."

"But that's not really the point, is it? And could you please stop that nerve-racking stalking about and settle somewhere?"

There was the sound of defiant movement. Antonia flinging herself into a chair, no doubt.

"I heard about her from Grandmother, you know. Couldn't you have at least written directly to me?"

"Under the circumstances, no."

"It was cruel."

Enrique said nothing. Then Antonia's voice came again.

"Did you have to do this to me? In this way?"

"What other way was there, *querida?*"

I waited through a deeper silence.

"How I feel is not to the point, obviously," Antonia went on bitterly. "The waning Fuente fortunes are about to be restored. The moldering Fuente castle can be propped up for another century or so. And your new wife can do all this with one or two scratches of the pen."

"Yes."

"But will she sign the papers?"

The change in Enrique's tone when he answered made the blood leap in my veins.

"She'll sign them. It will be my pleasure to see that she does."

I rose dizzily from my chair, ran back through the room, and fell on the bed. Feeling as chilled as though I had lain in a snowdrift, I reached for the eiderdown and pulled it up over me.

Afterward, when some warmth had come back, I knew a strange thing.

Enrique and Antonia had been speaking in Spanish, and I had understood every word they had said.

# Chapter 6

Shocked into immobility, I stared into the moon-drenched darkness.

*How had I come to know Spanish?*

My head began to throb, but I reasoned through the pain, *You could have learned Spanish anywhere. It's an ordinary enough accomplishment these days.*

The pain diminished, but did not go away entirely. Still I felt a strange peace, and I slept.

That night, for the first time, I dreamed a dream that was to recur many times in the weeks to come. And that first dreaming was like a cool compress on my head, so that the last of the pain left me as I slept.

The dream was a startlingly vivid one.

I saw myself standing in the doorway of a gray house with white steps. A man in a tan trench coat was running down the steps into a street dark with drifting rain.

The rain sparkled on the man's hair as he

hurried away from me. I tried to call out against his going, but I could make no sound. I went after him, running, too; but the space between us lengthened magically. I ran with the rain in my face and the wet strands of my hair blowing, and sadness in my heart.

At last, his back still to me, he disappeared around a corner in the glistening dark.

Tonight, as always afterward, I awakened from this dream stricken by my loss. Who was this man, who, as opposed to Enrique, brought such peace to me, even in the dreaming of him? A man so different from my "husband," a gentle comforting man, someone I knew I had loved very much in that other time, that other life, before the accident.

"Lisa?"

It was Enrique, knocking, then entering without waiting for an answer. "You called out."

"Not for you."

"No."

"I was dreaming."

Enrique crossed to my bed. "What were you dreaming?"

"Of a man," I answered maliciously.

"I see. Who is this man?"

"I don't know. I couldn't see his face. But

I'll recognize him when we meet again."

"But if you can't get to him, there's no way for the two of you to meet again, now is there?"

"I'll get to him."

Enrique recrossed the room. "Are you sure?" he asked, closing the door with deliberate softness as he left.


The next morning I awakened to find Anna propped beside my bed, staring down at me out of her one good eye.

"Good Lord!" I said, lurching upright.

Nita, who had been sitting in a chair near the bed, got up and came over to me. She was wearing a navy wool school uniform with a crisp white pinafore over it. "I thought you'd never wake up, *Tia* Lisa. And there's business to attend to."

"Well, let's attend to it, then."

"It's like this. I have to go to school, and you might be lonesome for California without me here. So I brought Anna to stay with you until I get back."

Greater love hath no man! "Thank you for letting Anna visit."

"Not at all, my dear," Nita answered, crossing to the door.

Shades of the English nanny. It was all I could do to keep the laughter back.

As Nita left the room, Feli arrived, anxiously balancing my breakfast tray. Seeing Nita, she was temporarily diverted, and began scolding in a stream of Spanish. *"Nita, está muy tarde . . ."*

"English, please," Nita interrupted, nodding significantly in my direction as she departed.

Feli, evidently flustered by this new responsibility, brought my tray and startled me by saying, "Good afternoon, señora."

This time I did laugh. "It's 'good morning' now, Feli."

*"Sí, señora,* 'Good morning' is *mejor."*

Especially since it's barely nine a.m. Cheered by my visitors, I began to eat with appetite.

"Is your breakfast *bueno, señora?"*

"Yes, wonderfully *bueno,* thank you."

Still Feli lingered, fidgeting. *"El señor dice que . . ."*

So the señor says, does he, I thought, annoyed. But I answered carefully, "Would you speak English, please?"

Feli, frowning with concentration, switched back to English.

"The señor says, when the señora finish, she must come to the room of books."

"Thank you for telling me, Feli."

I took a sip of coffee, swallowing with difficulty. How sick I was of Enrique's orders, and of his nearness.

After Feli left the room, I put down my cup, unable to eat now, newly desolate. Even that priceless gift from some dark corner of my amnesia, my remembering Spanish, seemed less important now.

This was ridiculous, of course. However I had come by it, the Spanish was an invaluable asset. It gave me a listening post into Enrique's secret frightening world. It stepped up my timetable for escape.

I thought of last night's dream. I belonged somewhere . . . hadn't I seen the house in my dream? . . . and I belonged to someone. I must get back to this place, to this other life, if there were to be any meaning in anything for me again.

But first I must escape Enrique. Could I do this?

Doubt was an emotion I couldn't afford. And anger and panic must be controlled, at all costs. How easy, if I gave in to these feelings, to appear hysterical and disturbed, a person to be watched ceaselessly by a solicitous husband.

Solicitous? At least until the papers were signed.

I got out of bed and dressed. I put on the brightest outfit I could muster, a red sweater and a navy and scarlet tweed skirt. I was determined to go down to Enrique with all flags flying.

Once I had reached the main floor, it took a minute to search out the library. I found it opposite the drawing room, off the central hallway.

I opened the door and stepped into a large room where a fire, smelling of burning pine logs, blazed in a stone fireplace at the far end of the room. Two other walls were crowded with books from floor to ceiling, and in the fourth wall was another row of tall windows. Through these windows I could see that the wind had come up again and had set a grove of aspen trees swaying like dancers.

"Good morning, Enrique."

"Ah, there you are, Lisa," he said pleasantly, getting to his feet. "There's something I wanted to see you about, but while we're talking I thought I might be showing you around the house a bit. You would like to have a look, wouldn't you?"

"Of course," I answered, trying to keep the interest out of my voice.

If I were to get away from here, I must first learn this place by heart, and I enjoyed the irony of having Enrique's assistance on my first reconnaissance trip.

As we went out of the room and down the hall, Enrique said, "You'll need something more in the way of a coat."

We had reached the front part of the house, where he opened the door of a closet under the stairs. He brought out two windbreakers and handed one of them to me.

I knew whose jacket was being offered. "It'll swallow me," I said, reluctant to wear it.

"No, it won't. Antonia is about your size."

I almost said, "Spare me her measurements, please," but I stopped myself in time.

This mental comment set me to wondering about Antonia and Enrique. Without question, Antonia was my "husband's" mistress. If Enrique had been bringing his bride home, certainly Antonia would have been long gone by now. There had been no indication in last night's conversation that she was leaving.

Further proof (had I needed it!) that I was a stranger, brought here for a purpose. My presence required no shift in relationships.

Thinking of that other Lisa, I hoped that I might at least be a specter at the feast, a sort of nerve-racking reminder of my dead counterpart.

I accepted the jacket, feeling as though I were donning the clothing of a particularly lethal enemy.

"Antonia asked me to apologize for not saying good-bye to you. She left this morning for La Coruña, and was gone before you got up."

"To stay?" I asked, wondering if I were mistaken about her not leaving. Antonia's inimical presence was one I could do without.

"Only for two or three days. She has an apartment there and goes in to see friends and shop."

I gave no sign of my disappointment.

We went out the front door and crossed the porch into the sunlight. A wind blew against us, cold, filled with tantalizing scents, a wind from the mountains.

Enrique paused on the edge of the porch, pointing. "There's the road we came up the other night, running parallel to the *ria* for part of the way, then past the *ria,* and finally curving on up the hill. This is the only good road up to the house."

"That's odd," I said, interested for reasons of my own.

"It is, but there's no other satisfactory access. The mountains begin a short distance back of the house, cutting us off on that side. From the dining-room side there's a road that runs down into the village, but that's a long way around to the main highway. And on the side where our bedrooms are there's nothing but a grove of trees, dropping off down to the *ria*. And, of course, beyond that is the sea."

A remote and inaccessible place, difficult to leave unnoticed. I suspected that I had been brought on this walk to make this fact clear to me.

Still, there had to be a way out, and I stubbornly set my mind to memorizing the landscape.

I looked at the road beside the *ria,* then, puzzled, at the *ria* itself. I was sure I'd heard it flowing the night we arrived, but now I saw only bogs and waving marsh grass and sky-tinted lakes.

"But I thought the *ria* was a river!"

"It is at high tide. Don't you remember, I explained all that? When the tide comes in the sea flows in over the marshes. The *rias* are drowned river valleys."

We stood, wind-buffeted, I avidly surveying all that lay before me. As we looked, the world changed around us. The wind came harder, carrying the smell of rain, and the light left the wings of the seagulls.

I studied the ria once more. A treacherous and lonely place to wander into. One would have to know the road that ran beside it very well, indeed, and more important, stay on this road.

"Ready?" Enrique asked at last. "Not bored, are you?"

"Not bored."

We struck out across the drive, around the front of the house, then down stone steps to the level of the dining room.

This was the direction I had faced into from the dining room yesterday, but the thin windows had restricted my view. Now, standing on the steps, I could see much farther. First there were the pine forests; beyond them, open cultivated land; and finally white fields marked off into squares by low dykes.

The white fields puzzled me, and when I asked about them, Enrique said, "Fields of salt. I'm a salt farmer."

"I'd like to see the salt fields," I replied, hoping for a closer view of the route into the village. "Could we take a look this morning?"

"No, it's too far to walk, I'm afraid."

Making my voice as offhand as possible, I asked, "And the village? How far?"

"Six kilometers. About three and a half miles. I'll take you in one day soon. Right now there's something more important I must show you."

I followed him around the corner to the back of the house. Below us lay a meadow dotted with walnut trees and surrounded by a lichen-covered wall. On the floor of the meadow, grass leaned before the wind, oxen moved through the grass, the copper bells around their necks tinkling with each step. Beyond the meadow were more mountains, rising gently here, but piled up steeply off to the left of the house.

We went down slate steps to the wall. Here, Enrique made a right angle turn toward the steeper hills, following a path parallel to the field.

Just at the edge of this field I saw something that gave me an unpleasant thrill. Several stone buildings, on posts, stood together. They were slitted for ventilation and there were crosses mounted on their peaked roofs. Each was the shape of an oversized coffin.

"What are those awful buildings? They look like sepulchers."

"What do you mean, 'sepulchers'?" Enrique replied, obviously annoyed by the comparison. "They're called *hórreos,* and they're silos for storing maize. On the small farms, bread is often stored there, or sometimes fruit."

He turned away and went on up the path, which was beginning to climb into the craggy hills. I followed, pausing only once to look back at the *hórreos*. They made a depressing sight, clustered there against the darkening sky, their sides streaked by years of rain.

I started after Enrique, my breath growing ragged as the steepness of the path increased.

"Almost there."

"Why is this thing you want to show me so important?"

I thought he hesitated. "Because there's something here that you must know about."

I stumbled, shooting loose gravel from beneath my feet; he turned back, leaned down and hauled me up, and we came together onto the crest of the first low hill.

I looked about me, not liking the desolation of the place. The day was darkening, and a mist was rising from the *ria* and the wind-swept estuaries. I moved into the lee of a boulder to shelter from the wind, and thought what a melancholy land Galicia was, a place where the rain fell endlessly and mist drifted like smoke across the moors.

"What was it you wanted to show me?" I asked, anxious to be gone.

"Glance around and tell me what you see."

"Just a hill, rather bare except for some stiff, kinky-looking vegetation. Right in the middle of the hill there's a funny indentation with slanting sides and bushes at the bottom."

Enrique came over, caught me by the wrist and led me up to the edge of the indentation.

"Now listen closely. This 'funny' indentation has a large hole at its bottom. You can't see the hole because bushes grow around its edges. These mountains are limestone and they're honeycombed with caves where the crust has fallen in."

A single drop of rain pinged on a rock behind me. I longed to pull my hand away from Enrique's grasp but his fingers circled my wrist like a hot wire. We stood, staring down at the spot where the hole was.

"You must be very careful," he went on softly, "because that hole is large enough for an adult to fall through, and from the hole there's a two hundred foot drop into a subterranean river."

# Chapter 7

Another raindrop hit my face and ran down my cheek. I pulled away from Enrique.

"Why, for heaven's sake, haven't you covered this hole?" I asked.

"Good God, I'd spend the rest of my life patching holes in the hills. These mountains are cracked with natural fractures and with the heavy rainfall dissolving the limestone, the fissures widen and blocks of the mountain crumble away, leaving caves. More rain and some of the caves fall in at the crest. They're everywhere, these danger spots, but most of the families have lived here for generations and know all about them."

That takes care of everyone but me, I thought.

Could I ever get out of this place? To the west and north of the house lay the treacherous *ria*, bordered by a single road; here to the south, the mountains, riddled with dangerous open caves; to the east, the village.

To get to the village unseen, I must slip away at night and walk six kilometers. It was a frightening prospect. Certainly there would be no such walks until I had learned my way and learned it well.

"Now, no more about the caves," Enrique said, his voice growing warm and pleasant again.

He was making one of his chameleon changes, focusing the full force of his charm on me, a charm that, with his blazing good looks, was formidable. Fortunately, I was impervious.

I watched him through narrowed eyes. I knew exactly what was coming.

"Do you remember the papers I spoke to you about on the plane, Lisa?"

"I remember," I answered coldly.

"Before you sign, I want to explain about them."

"Yes, do," I answered, the coldness in my voice deepening.

"I have some property near Anaheim in Southern California, remnants of a Spanish land grant that have been in my family for generations. There are two depleted oil wells, just about done for, on the land, so the income hasn't amounted to much for a long time now. But it was enough for one person to live on. When we became engaged, I made it over to you."

I listened with attention, weighing every word against his revealing conversation with Antonia last night, on guard against his deftness.

"Wasn't that a rather unusual thing for you to do?"

"Perhaps. But the oil income was a small gift, after all. A kind of insurance for you. If anything had happened to me before we were married, you would have been very much alone, very much on your own resources. Your uncle seems to have little enough himself, and you and he were not close, in any case."

"My family left nothing at all?" I asked carefully.

"A Cadillac, a Porsche, and some debts. Your mother and father lived in the Generalissimo area of Madrid, in an extremely expensive house. Rented."

All this was said with a practiced ease that set my body tingling with apprehension. But I sat motionless, listening, knowing that we hadn't reached the heart of the matter yet.

"The situation has changed on the Anaheim property." Enrique seemed less sure of himself now, to be choosing his words with care. "We've had a staggering offer for this land. A real estate developer wants to buy it for a housing project. But there's a time limit to the offer. I must give my answer within the next thirty days. I suppose the developer has an eye on other large tracts, as well. Time is running out."

In more ways than one, I thought. Your time may be running out as far as I'm concerned, too. But of course Enrique knew this.

I realized, with considerable satisfaction, that my "husband" must measure the crucial days ahead by two separate clocks, each independently ticking away the minutes toward possible disaster.

I was the more threatening of the two because of my mysterious timing. I had to be dealt with first. I suppressed a shudder as a raw wind blew against me, lifting my hair with wet fingers.

"My family's interest has revived since the land has become so valuable. And the original reason for my giving you the property is now invalid, of course, since we're married and you're home with me. Although the land was in my name, in the light of its increased value, my family feels that it should be considered as estate property, and sold for the benefit of all of us."

"And it cannot be sold without my signature?"

"No."

The rain had begun in earnest. Enrique seemed not to notice it.

"I'd like to put the major portion of our share into the salt operation that I showed you. But to make the salt farming really successful, expansion is necessary, and a salt distillation plant in the village, essential."

No mention of Antonia's bitter reference to the need for bolstering up failing family fortunes. Evidently there would be sufficient funds for everything, for everyone. A great deal of money, then.

The bleak wind blew again, its glacial caresses lingering across me.

How remarkably clever Enrique had been throughout; but the cleverest people make mistakes. Enrique's explanation of how the California land had left his possession sounded contrived, too unlikely.

Lisa, not Enrique, had owned this valuable property, I decided. And Lisa, as his bride, would undoubtedly have listened to Enrique's husbandly advice and signed happily and quickly, taking advantage of this "staggering" offer, an offer that she may have little understood or cared about, but one that would have given Enrique access to the fortune needed and longed for.

But Lisa had died on her wedding night, before there had been time to sign anything, and being as young as she was, had probably died intestate. Still, Enrique would be the automatic legatee, would he not?

But a death of this kind certainly would raise many questions. Other heirs to hunt out. Possibly all lost papers would have to be retraced. Had the marriage license been destroyed in the accident? Wouldn't doctors and nurses concerned with the crash have to be reassembled, requestioned?

Even if there had been a will leaving everything to Enrique, probate took time. The courts, like the mills of the gods, grind slowly, and this litigation might involve both American and Spanish courts.

It was not inconceivable that Lisa's money could be tied up for years . . . and here was a once-in-a-lifetime offer, one that stood to restore the diminishing fortunes of the proud Fuentes . . . but only thirty days in which to take advantage of this offer.

And there had been I, in the same hospital with Enrique, the type and approximate age of his dead wife, my parents killed in the crash, my memory totally gone, and no one to identify me but a cousin I hadn't seen in five years.

Risky, for Enrique, yes. But the stakes were high, and for a man who was daring enough, worth the risk. I considered my "husband" such a man.

How had he brought it off, I wondered, frightened by the thoroughness of his machinations.

Perhaps it had not been so difficult, after all.

Attractive and assured, every inch the distraught husband, he could have guided the confused doctors and police through the identifications to the conclusions he had wanted them to reach. Best of all, I had had no American driver's license, no identifying photograph.

He'd been lucky there; but still there *I* was. Still to be convinced. Surprisingly, he'd managed this too, at least long enough to get me out of the country, and tucked away in a remote Galician village. His village.

How had he done this, when my very blood and bones had shouted back at me that I was not his wife?

I decided that it was his cleverness in piecing together a rather special past for me; a past that I guessed was not entirely false. He must have learned a great deal about me, sitting beside my bed, day after day, deliberately listening to my unconscious revelations.

Playing expertly upon my lonely uncertainty as an amnesic, still he must have told the truth wherever he could, so that when I stumbled over bits of truth about myself, doubts would subside.

Those days in Spain as a child must have belonged to me, just as Enrique had said; they explained my understanding of Spanish.

But I guessed that my later history came almost entirely from the dead girl's past. There had been a Lisa Stephens who had gone to Stanford, met and married Enrique. But I knew in my heart that I was not that girl.

I moved over under a tree and sat down on a wet, moss covered log. Enrique followed and stood looking down at me.

"Well?" he asked.

I glanced away, trying to steady myself. Now that the moment of refusal had come, I felt cloudy with terror, wondering if I could hold out against this man.

I must hold out. Until I could make my break for freedom, I had to guarantee my safety inside my prison. The only way I could do this was to refuse to sign anything. As long as my signature was needed, I was not expendable.

A frown was drawing Enrique's brows together. "Will you sign the papers or not?"

A small, painful gasp escaped me. "No."

I saw the flash of incredulity in his face (had he thought to soften me up so easily?) and then I felt the anger gathering in him. He reached down, closed his fingers painfully on my chin, and pressed hard against the bones of my face.

I pulled against his grasp. He released me abruptly, swung away, and stood staring off toward the sea. The rain came faster, falling in large, clear drops that darkened his clothes. I sat huddled on my log, wondering what he'd do next.

To my surprise, he left without another word, half-running down the steep path, disappearing and reappearing, as the path wound in and out among trees bright with rain.

I hadn't expected such a swift departure. I got to my feet and started down, too. The entire mountain seemed in motion now, with wind moving under the ferns and sighing in the wet trees. Puddles of water threw back shifting reflections, and in the distance I could hear the wilder movement of the sea, breaking along the shore with a sound like shattering glass.

By the time I had reached the slate wall Enrique was out of sight and the rain was falling steadily. I averted my eyes passing the *hórreos,* realizing how much I disliked the smell of damp stone. Off to the left of the house I saw an elderly gardener clipping a hedge, working away in the rain as though it didn't exist.

As I passed along the meadow fence, the rain came harder. I ran for a big chestnut tree that stood by itself between the meadow and the house. The tree, with the wind scattering raindrops out of its lower branches, made the dampest of shelters, but it offered some protection and I remained under it, waiting for a slackening in the downpour.

Huddling there, I studied the back of the house. Here all three levels were in view, including the servants' entrances on the ground floor, and at the second level, a long terrace surrounded by a low wall lined with pots of fiery geraniums.

This terrace was reached by a stone staircase, and I decided I would re-enter the house through this back way; I was sure the door from the terrace led onto the landing above the dining room. From there I would have no difficulty finding my way down the central hall and back to my bedroom.

I saw the door onto the terrace burst open and a small figure come flying out, and shoot off toward the steps.

Nita. Evidently she had spotted me under my tree and decided to meet me, in total disregard of the rain. I called to her to go back but the wind caught the words and carried them away. Oddly, at that instant, Nita did pause; it was almost as though she'd been jerked backward on an invisible string.

I knew that someone standing back in the shadows of the dark doorway had commanded her to stop; she obeyed instantly. In my short acquaintance with Nita, I had summed her up as strong-willed and not easily diverted from her private schemes, so I wondered who had managed to turn her back into the house so deftly.

Not ten seconds later I heard a sharp, hard crack and saw a spurt of sodden leaves fly up into the air a few feet away from me.

I stared down at the ruffled leaves in sick surprise; there was no problem identifying the sound. It was the deadly passage of a rifle bullet, coming from somewhere behind me.

Unable to think, blown before a shameful panic, I tore out into the open, running toward the house, falling in the muddy grass, getting up, running again.

At last, I stepped into a shallow hole and fell forward on the ground with a jolt. I remained there on my hands and knees for a humiliating moment; but the fall had cleared my mind and I got to my feet with some semblance of dignity, realizing that if someone were trying to shoot me, my wild dash into the open was probably the best move I could have made. Now my assailant would have to gun me down in front of a houseful of people going back and forth past innumerable windows.

Still it was a hard and prickly journey walking in full view across the lawns to the terrace. But my common sense, in abeyance for some time now, was beginning to function again.

Poor farmers with meager tables probably hunted these hills, so the bullet could have been a stray one. I wanted to think this, and it made sense. Otherwise, why had my assailant missed? I had been a bright and stationary target under my tree. Someone wanting to kill me had only to choose a spot at close range and take all the time he needed with his aim. I saw no reason why he should not have hit me.

Reaching the terrace steps I paused, held in thrall by my own thoughts. The rifle shot could have been a stray one, or it could have been something else altogether; a deliberate near miss, a warning to do as I was told.

But I had not definitely refused to sign the papers until this afternoon, so that no one knew about this refusal.

No one but Enrique.

# Chapter 8

The door into the house led onto the back landing of the main floor, just as I had expected; and under the spectral tinkling of the chandelier, I crossed this landing to the far door and went down the hall.

I hoped to get to my room without meeting anyone, so I moved swiftly through the silent house. I had reached the foot of the main staircase, when a door opened and a voice halted me.

"Lisa."

It was the grandmother, standing in the doorway of the drawing room. She seemed less formidable this morning, dressed simply in gray cashmere and leaning on her cane; but the hooded eyes missed nothing.

"My dear, you're wet through."

"I went for a walk and the rain surprised me."

"Yes, the rains come suddenly in Galicia.

But now you must change, I think. Before you become chilled."

In spite of her seeming preoccupation with my soaked clothes, she kept staring at my face.

"Are you quite certain you are all right?"

I knew I was pale, and it seemed to me that the frown drawing her brows together might be one of genuine anxiety. Rashly, in my alarm and loneliness, I almost told her what had happened. Just in time I remembered that unseen person who had called Nita back into the safety of the house a few seconds before the rifle shot had split the air beside me.

I would tell the grandmother nothing, I decided.

"I'm perfectly all right, thank you."

Still she hesitated. "Perhaps you'd like a tray in your room? You see, Enrique is rarely in for lunch and Antonia is away . . . so Carlos and I often take a light meal in our apartments under these circumstances . . ."

"Yes, that would be lovely," I answered, longing to be gone from her.

"I'll have Feli bring something to your room, then."

I thanked her again.

"Not at all," she replied formally, but as I started up the stairs she spoke once more. "I hope you won't find it dull and lonely here when Enrique is away."

It was all I could do to hold back a shout of hysterical laughter, but I answered calmly enough. "Oh, no, I'll not find it dull here, I'm sure."

"Perhaps you'd like to drive into the village this afternoon and look around? It's an interesting little place and the church is very old . . ."

I stared at her in disbelief. Just the chance I'd longed for.

"Yes, indeed, I'd like that."

"Nita, who has been on half holiday this morning, is dressing for school now and will be going into the village for her afternoon classes in a few minutes. At five-thirty the gardener will be driving in again, to fetch her. If you are ready at that time, he will be glad to take you as well. He will be waiting for you at the front entrance."

"Thank you. I'll be ready at five-thirty."

Turning away from her again, I ran up the stairs. I could scarcely believe my good fortune. This dreadful day wasn't to end in total defeat after all.

Reaching my room, I threw off my sopping clothes and climbed into a steaming bath, where I lay thinking troubled thoughts. I was still shaken from my near disaster this morning and trying to make sense of it. Accident or warning? If it were a warning, it was a heart-stopping one. But far from frightening me into signing the papers, it had hardened my resolve not to do so. My stalker might shoot at me forever, but it was obvious he had no wish to kill me.

He wanted papers signed and the dead don't write.

So I was back to the old proposition that I would remain safe as long as I refused to fall in with Enrique's plans. I had to let it go at that, because there were other urgent things to consider now.

What was the grandmother's role in all this? She seemed to have no concern about my going into the village. Either she was not in on the scheme to keep me here against my will, or she did know and thought there was no risk involved in letting me go into the town.

Perhaps my story had already been carefully spread among the villagers. I could almost hear Enrique, in his relaxed charming way, explaining the accident, my memory loss . . . and, worst of all, the possibility of my relapsing into a fugue and attempting flight. Would it be too much to ask of his old friends to keep an eye on me? To let him know if I were seen leaving, etc.

I climbed out of the tub. My bath had grown cold, and even with the warm towel from the rack I found it hard to rub the cold feeling away.

After lunch and a nap, I awakened at five sharp and saw that Feli had come in and taken my tray without my knowing. In spite of my disturbing morning, I had slept deeply; but I was unrefreshed. Still, the excitement of getting out of the house and into the village brought me to my feet in a nervous rush.

I went to the closet and indifferently chose clothes for my jaunt, even though all of the new things Enrique had selected for me were attractive.

I put on an Irish tweed wraparound skirt, the color of cream, a heavy silk shirt, and a sleeveless fisherman's sweater. These clothes, right in California, were much too light for such a day, in such a place, and bore mute testimony to the brief Americanization of Enrique. This was also true of the scarlet trench coat that I slipped into.

Here against the dripping landscape and the somberness of a Galician village, I would stand out like the burning bush in the Bible.

By five-thirty I was on the front porch,

watching tattered clouds sail the sky. In the distance the *ria* was still drifting with rain, but here an occasional shaft of sunlight lighted a pine or picked up the orange glow of wild poppies growing on a stone wall.

I hadn't long to wait before an ancient black Mercedes rolled up the drive and stopped in front of me. The car was beautifully kept, polished to mirror brightness, and the sound of its engine was no more than a silky whisper.

As I started down the steps, a young man got out of the car, came around to my side and opened the back door for me.

"Good afternoon, señora," he said, in heavily accented English. "My name is Alfredo Garcia."

"Good afternoon, Alfredo."

We studied each other. His dark eyes flicked over me arrogantly, in the manner of the Spanish male taking in any reasonably attractive female in shouting distance. I couldn't guess what conclusion he came to, but I, for my part, found him distinctly puzzling. This was not the gardener I had seen at a distance on my walk with Enrique this morning. He had been a much older man.

I supposed Alfredo could be an under-gardener, but he didn't look to be an under-anything. Although he wore the clothes of the Spanish working man, rusty black suit coat and trousers and an aging white shirt buttoned at the neck, his dark cap sat at a jaunty angle and he had the assurance and easy manners of someone who had been exposed to a wider kind of life. He looked young and tough, more like a guerrilla fighter than a gardener.

As he helped me into the car and went back to the driver's seat, I watched him, finding him disturbing; and this dimmed the excitement of my trip to the village.

Finally, I gave up and began questioning him hesitantly. "You're not the gardener, are you? I haven't seen you here before, I think."

Amused dark eyes met mine in the rearview mirror. "No, señora, I'm not the gardener. Isabella, the cook, is my mother. I was born here and I grew up with Enrique."

He still hadn't told me who he was. But in the end I knew.

He was Enrique's friend and trusted lieutenant. He was also my guard, taking me for a cautious airing outside the prison walls.

The car moved down the drive and turned toward the village, along a road that barely allowed for passing. Stone walls, half smothered in blackberry vines and baby ferns, ran along either side of the road and trees arched over us, closing out the sky.

I sank back in the corner of the seat and watched the dripping vines flash past, depressed by a number of things, including my escort.

In a short time, however, we came out of the avenue of trees onto a broad plain where the sunlight fell across fields of maize still shining with rain. This was the first glimpse of sun I'd had in some time; and when I saw a flight of swallows lift from a clump of bushes and head skyward in a burst of song, my spirits lifted with them, and I looked about me with interest.

Here on the open land, we began passing stone farmhouses with doors and windows so tightly closed that they appeared permanently sealed. Grape arbors, supported by hand-hewn slate posts, ran across the fronts of these silent farms, darkening them still more. One would have guessed the houses deserted had it not been for masses of geraniums glowing like hot coals in the arbors; and I marveled at people who sought such darkness.

These must be tenant farms of the Fuente estate, and I wanted to ask Alfredo if this were so; but still angry at being sent out on my excursion under guard, I remained silent.

In a short time the face of the land

changed once more. The salt fields. They were all about us now, outlined by salt-encrusted dykes. Nearby lay shallow valleys with streams rising in their centers; these streams, running red with dark red soil, were channeled into the dyked fields.

I sat forward, curious.

Glancing up, I saw Alfredo watching me in the rearview mirror again, veiled eyes taking in my curiosity.

"Fields of salt, señora," he said in a cold voice.

"Yes, I see," I answered, matching the coldness. But another prod from my curiosity made me ask, "How does it happen that the salt is on the surface? I thought it came from underground mines ."

"In this part of Galicia, which borders on Asturias, the earth is very salty, and streams rising from underground springs come up into these valleys, bringing the salt from below. On the Fuente land, Enrique and I have directed these streams into dyked fields. Here the water eventually evaporates, leaving the salt. Then we collect the salt and send it away to be made pure."

"Enrique and I," he'd said. So Alfredo was some sort of partner in the salt operation.

Highly uneasy again, I remembered something else. Alfredo had not used the customary "Don" when referring to Enrique. This indicated a degree of friendship, a degree of equality, unusual between master and servant. But Alfredo had been born and raised on the estate, he'd said. He and Enrique must have been friends since childhood.

Certainly, Alfredo was no ordinary servant and I had recognized this by his attitude alone. What I hadn't known, and what frightened me now, was the fact of his involvement in the salt operation. And I thought I now understood something that had confused me from the time I had first stepped into the car: Alfredo's antagonism toward me.

Whether he was a full partner in the business or not, he was obviously vitally interested and involved in it, and it followed that he would not take kindly to resistance in signing papers that would release money needed for rescuing and expanding the salt operation. As Enrique's confidant and associate, I was certain he had been advised of this resistance from the moment my "husband" and I had arrived in Galicia.

A tough-minded man, this Alfredo. I saw him as narrow, inflexible, determined.

I was up against not one but two ruthless, ambitious men who evidently felt no compunction about holding me prisoner until I had signed the papers they wanted signed.

And then, what?

I shrank back in my corner, lost in one of the darkest periods I'd known since coming to Galicia.

Swamped in self-distrust, I sat staring at Alfredo's powerful shoulders. Then he moved and something in the movement, the arrogant tilt of the head perhaps, sent a shaft of anger through me, and I rallied. Even if I failed in the end, I would give my sinister guardians a few battle scars to remember me by.

So instead of cowering in my corner I sat upright once more and rode into the village feeling hot of cheek and sparkly of eye. The Mercedes, moving easily over the uneven cobblestones of a narrow street, came to a stop beside a plaza.

Alfredo got out of the car and opening the door for me, said formally, "It will be a few minutes before Nita is finished with her lessons. Meanwhile, would the señora care to stroll in the village?"

The señora would not only care to stroll in the village but right on through it and out the other side, I thought viciously. But I kept all betraying thoughts to myself.

In spite of the correctness of voice and

manner, Alfredo had infused a subtle impertinence into every word, and I was certain this was deliberate. I managed a remote "Thank you" as I got out of the car; and sustained by fresh anger, I walked away, knowing that I was watched at every step.

# *Chapter 9*

I soon forgot Alfredo, however, in looking over the village. It was a small hilly place dominated by a cathedral of the same honey-colored stone as Enrique's house. The cathedral looked down on the plaza which contained swaying ash trees and a cracked stone fountain. The plaza was the center of the town and cobblestoned streets fanned out from it, twisting off into the hills, dead-ending against stone retaining walls.

An intricate, bewildering little town. One would have to be well acquainted with its winding streets to pass through easily.

Crossing over from the plaza, I made my way down the first street I came to. Here the shops were small; and smells, cold and ancient, drifted out from the dark of their open doorways. A boy on a bicycle rode by and I smiled at him, expecting friendliness. Instead, I received only a curious stare, and I passed on, shaken.

Near the next corner, two women of indeterminate age sat sewing on camp stools in front of a lacy, iron gate. It was necessary to pass within a few feet of them, and I knew it was impossible for them to miss me. When I came abreast of them I looked in their direction; they ducked their heads and pretended not to see me.

What was the matter with the people in this awful place? And why had I assumed they would be friendly? I didn't know why, of course, because I had no specific memory of the Spain I must have known as a child; the assumption was no more than an echo of a memory.

I turned and started back toward the plaza, and on the way passed an old man with a harsh, forbidding face. Afraid of another cruel snub, I looked away. This was just as well because at that moment I felt a single, shameful tear run down my cheek.

I hurried on, recrossed the street, and reached a corner of the plaza again just as the cathedral bells began ringing through the dying sunlight, filling the town with sound. I stood caught in the lovely clamor, suddenly taut with expectancy, almost remembering after all, because of the bells.

The moment passed; the memory refused to come and I was left with my frustration and more echoes.

Still, in a way I knew I did remember. The sights and sounds around me were familiar.

How many times had I watched the dusk moving in across saffron-colored rooftops or seen women all in black, carrying baskets over their arms, hurrying off down shadowy streets? And I'd watched lights wink on in sidewalk cafes, as they were doing now in the cafe across the plaza; and I'd seen carved doors, like the doors in the building next to the cathedral, open to spill chattering, jostling boys onto the street.

Yes, I had seen all this before, but I had seen these things in another part of Spain. I stood, lonely and afraid, knowing that my town had been warm even in late afternoon, filled with light and whispering winds, the stones in the walls just cooling, the faces in the street ready for laughter.

Not like Enrique's chilling hostile village.

Out of the corner of my eye, I could see Alfredo, half a block away, watching me. Wind shook the tree above me and a spray of raindrops fell on my head and ran down inside my coat collar.

Too depressing, and worse yet my will to explore and make escape plans had temporarily bogged down under the weight of this depression.

I wished Nita would come.

Then I heard a joyous shriek from somewhere behind me and Nita's voice calling to me through the subsiding bells. "*Tia* Lisa. I'm here."

I swung around to find her tearing down the street toward me, her black braids flying. In the next instant I was staggered by a fiercely affectionate embrace and a breathless, "I'm glad to see you, *Tia*."

"I believe you," I replied, steadying myself and kissing a cold rosy cheek.

She stood back, grabbed my hand and said in her best nanny voice, "I didn't know you were coming, but since you're here I'll show you around, my dear."

"Well, thanks very much, my dear, but aren't we due home soon?" I asked, anxious to be gone from this hateful village. One way and another I had taken quite a battering today, and I thought I might do better at facing so much concentrated hostility another time.

Before Nita could answer, Alfredo interfered, of course. He was standing beside the car watching everything and he cupped his hands around his mouth and called, "Nita, it grows late . . ."

"I'll see to him," Nita said, and she turned and ran back to Alfredo.

I watched them conferring, thinking that

Nita had met her match in that cold fish. But she was back almost immediately. "Forty-five minutes." I shook my head in wonder.

"Forty-five minutes will give me time to introduce you to a few friends," she said, taking my hand again and starting me off around the plaza.

I drew in a shaky breath, dreading my guided tour, but determined to go through with it rather than disappoint Nita.

Under Nita's magic sponsorship, I soon discovered that I was faring differently. Her "few friends" turned out to be everyone in town. People appeared from nowhere, drifting out of dark shops, or opening shutters to lean across casements and call, "*¡Hola! Juanita!*"

Nita introduced me with great politeness and the introductions were acknowledged in kind. There were still covert glances; but the narrowed eyes opened now and looked into mine, and somber faces lighted with smiles.

"You must say *'Encantada'* when I introduce you," Nita instructed me. "That means you're enchanted."

Which I was . . . enchanted with my guide, at least.

Our progress around the square was

pleasant and our first major stop a dim little store selling meats.

Here we met the butcher and saw three dressed suckling pigs, hanging from the ceiling, swinging rhythmically. Then on to the *farmacia* to meet the druggist and weigh on his scales (Nita's treat . . . total outlay: two grubby *pesetas* fished out of a pinafore pocket); on past an alley where the smell of rancid olive oil made my nostrils quiver with distaste; then by a *frutería* with open stalls of polished apples and stacks of oranges in golden pyramids.

We turned the last corner, ending up at the sidewalk cafe. Here I was introduced to the waiter, and Nita settled herself in a chair and recommended the hot chocolate. She also suggested, delicately, that I pay, the bald fact being that since treating me to my weight and a card with my fortune on it, she was out of funds.

"Fair enough," I said smiling, opening my bag before I remembered that there would be no money. I had not needed money since I had come away with Enrique, and I couldn't have brought myself to ask for any if I had.

But there *was* money in my purse, a neatly folded hundred *peseta* note stuck into a side pocket. As I sat staring down at the note I felt a coolness creep along my skin. Once again, Enrique was thinking miles ahead of me. I was always to be supplied with some money, evidently, so that the Fuente family stood in no danger of being embarrassed by my turning up in the village dead broke. But I was never to be allowed more than enough for a small purchase.

I snapped my bag closed, hating Enrique for the silent and terrible message he had sent me. He was saying in effect, "You had forgotten about money, hadn't you? But you must see that without it there's no way out."

And of course there wasn't.

My agitation must have shown in my face because I looked up to find Nita watching me anxiously. Still determined not to spoil her outing, I smiled and said, "Two hot chocolates it is. We're in the chips."

Nita dissolved into relieved laughter. "Oh, *Tia* Lisa, you say the most peculiar things."

"No doubt about it, I'm an odd one," I answered a little wildly. "Order up."

Nita called the waiter and the two of them went into conference.

It was while this was going on that the American turned up. He was a pleasant-looking young man who simply appeared at our table, and pausing beside the empty chair, said, "I beg your pardon, but I heard you speaking and I wondered . . ." He stopped in confusion. "Are you an American by any chance?"

"An American, yes . . ."

"My name is Edward Meredith. I haven't been in Spain long and it was such a treat hearing English for a change. . . . I hope you don't mind my coming over like this."

I took a look at Edward Meredith and decided that I liked what I saw. He was tall, with red hair and a bony freckled face that would have been plain without the disarming smile. I liked his eyes, humorous, thick-lashed, and gray behind his horn-rimmed glasses.

I continued to look at him, while a fiery excitement rose in me. Here was another American, one new to Spain, a person totally detached from the Fuente family and therefore outside their powerful reach. Edward Meredith might prove to be the lifeline that I had longed so desperately for, my way out.

I knew my excitement was showing in my face, in the color that made my cheeks hot. Trying to control an excess of cordiality, I said, "My name is Lisa," and here I stumbled slightly, "Fuente. This is my niece, Juanita Fuente."

"It's a great pleasure," he replied, looking shyer than ever.

Nita got to her feet, and made a slight curtsy. "How do you do?"

The performance was flawless (the beautiful manners of the Fuentes obviously began early); but the usual bubbling warmth that accompanied all of Nita's actions was embarrassingly absent.

Edward had no way of knowing this, and I could see that he was much struck by Nita's welcome.

"We're having some chocolate. Won't you join us?" I asked, trying to keep the eagerness out of my voice.

"Yes, indeed, I'd like that," he answered, sitting down. "But you must be my guests. And I think I'll make mine coffee."

The waiter returned and Edward ordered for us, in the most atrocious Spanish I'd ever heard.

"And what brings you to Spain, Mr. Meredith?" I asked.

"Edward, please."

"Edward, then, and you must call me 'Lisa.' Are you here for long?"

I knew I was rushing things, but I couldn't stop. As the excitement heightened in me, so did a disagreeable sense of urgency. I had to let this man know I needed help and with

Nita close by I saw no way of doing this.

"I expect to be in Galicia for a short time only. I'm a mining geologist on a field trip."

Only a few days, perhaps, and it was unlikely I would run into Edward again. I must get my call for help through to him before we separated this evening or he would be lost to me for good.

Glancing about me unhappily, I realized that the cafe had filled with men; they had come for their evening glass of wine. The sidelong glances had begun again, this time not only directed at me but at Edward, as well. Added to this was the problem of Nita. Wearing a rakish chocolate mustache, she sat between us, missing nothing.

"Have you been in Galicia long?" Edward asked hesitatingly.

"My . . . my family lives near here, outside the village," I answered, threading my way. I certainly didn't want Edward to know I was married until I could tell him how I was married.

I could feel my heart beating out the passing seconds and still I could think of no way of breaking through to him.

"Nita," I said rather desperately, "I think we've overstayed our time. Would you go and find Alfredo and tell him that we'll be starting back soon?"

"There's no need to go and find Alfredo. He's standing at the bar."

I half turned in my chair to discover the ubiquitous Alfredo, his eyes fixed on me. When he had entered the cafe I didn't know. He was leaning against the bar drinking wine; and he seemed in no hurry or to have any plans for returning home. This was strange, and it added to my growing feeling of anxiety.

"Would you go and tell him anyway, please?" I persisted.

Nita got to her feet and started toward the bar. It was then that I realized that under cover of the evening wine ritual, Edward and I were being watched on all sides, not with the frozen reserve I'd met with earlier from the villagers, but with alertness and suspicion.

I understood this. Everyone in the village knew by now that I was Enrique's wife and here I sat talking to a strange American, my cheeks flushed, my face filled with excitement. And I had obviously unloaded Nita so that Edward and I could talk alone.

I knew I had lost all the ground I'd gained on my tour with Nita but there was no help for that; and I was already taken up with a more pressing question.

Would this man, not knowing me, believe my fantastic story?

"Edward," I said in a low voice, "please help me."

"Help you?" he answered, startled. Then, after looking into my face for a moment, he said, "All right. How?"

Here was a man who accepted on faith, evidently, and did his checking afterward. My spirits soared.

"I must get out of Spain . . ." I began, but my next words were lost in the noise of an accelerating sports car as it shot down the street toward the cafe. Someone was in a tearing hurry to get to the village. The roar increased as the car reached us and swung into the curb.

The engine was cut abruptly, the door of the car flew open, and a man stepped out.

"Good evening, Lisa," Enrique said in his coldest voice.

# Chapter 10

How had he found me, and how had he known about Edward? Had Alfredo called him?

No matter. Enrique was capable of thwarting me without any help from anyone.

He stood at our table now and I looked straight at him, letting the raw hate I was feeling show in my face. He looked back at me, his eyes narrowed to arctic, ice-blue slits.

Nita, uncommonly subdued, said faintly, "*¡Hola! Tio.*"

He glanced down at her blindly, but the force of his attention centered on Edward and me; and the air crackled with tension.

Edward rose awkwardly to his feet.

"Mr. Meredith, Señor Fuente," I said in a sullen voice, determined not to use the words "my husband."

The men shook hands and Enrique,

making no move to sit down, keeping Edward standing too, said coolly, "I'm glad Lisa ran into you, Mr. Meredith. My wife," he paused, bearing down on the two words, "hasn't been in Galicia long, and I'm sure it's a pleasure for her to have a chance to visit with another American."

"I think the pleasure was mainly mine," Edward answered, with a friendly smile.

But his gray eyes, behind his glasses, were alert and wary. He was clearly surprised and feeling his way about in this situation, trying to reconcile a personable husband and a beguiling niece with my cry for help; but the wariness showed he wasn't allowing himself to be taken in by appearances, perhaps for chauvinistic reasons or because my sense of desperation had come through to him silently. In any case, I could feel him strongly on my side.

"Will you be in Galicia long, Mr. Meredith?"

Enrique, standing straight and easy beside his chair, seemed indifferent to the answer; but I received the horrifying impression of a man crouched and waiting, listening with every nerve for the answer.

"It's difficult to say. I'm here investigating some mining possibilities. I'm staying in a place called Lugo. But I haven't quite finished looking over this area."

Briefly, Edward's gaze met mine. "I thought I'd return here early next week, perhaps."

I glanced away, wondering if Edward were trying to set up another meeting for us, feeling a rush of hope that this might be true. I couldn't be certain, but I could come to the village to meet Nita each afternoon, on the chance that he might return.

"I hope we meet again," Edward went on.

"Yes, indeed," Enrique said, his eyes chilling to a deeper blue. Then he turned away to Nita. "Well past your *merienda* and your bedtime, *querida mia*. We must get you home."

Nita and I rose to our feet, I, reluctantly. The good-byes were brief. I didn't dare look directly at Edward again, but our parting handshake was marked by an encouraging pressure from his big freckled hand.

"I think I'll ride with you and *Tia* Lisa, *Tio*," Nita said, as we walked away from the table.

"I think you won't. You'll ride with Alfredo, if you please."

Nita turned toward her uncle ready to protest, but one quelling glance from Enrique silenced her.

"March," he commanded grimly.

115

Nita marched, her small back rigid with indignation.

"Do you have to be so hateful?" I asked as I got into the car.

"Do you?" he countered.

He started the engine and the car slid away from the curb, accelerating as we moved off down the dimly lighted street. Soon we were out of the village and going at what seemed to me a dangerous speed on the open road. The rain had started again, falling in a fine mist, and the salt fields looked silver in the wet starlight. Here and there a lamp glowed behind closed shutters in a farmhouse; and behind us, in the village, the cathedral bells marked the hour .

Enrique was driving much too fast, his eyes narrowed against the luminous dark. I, determined not to break the silence, clung nervously to the door handle as we sped along.

My nervousness increased as we approached the tunnel of trees, but here, to my relief, Enrique began slowing down.

"How did you meet Meredith?" he asked abruptly.

"He came to our table and introduced himself."

"Are you sure you hadn't known him before?"

I turned and stared at Enrique's rigid profile. What could he mean by such an odd question?

"Certainly not. Why should Edward pretend to be a stranger, if he were not? And if he had done such an odd thing, since, as you're so fond of pointing out, I'm an amnesic, I couldn't know, could I?"

Enrique sent me a glittering, sidelong glance. "Sometimes I wonder," he said, "just what you do remember."

I faced away to the window, tingling with alarm. I couldn't think what would make Enrique say such a thing unless he'd somehow discovered that I knew Spanish. That was impossible; I had been so careful. Perhaps with that uncanny perception of his, he had felt a secret in me. But he couldn't know what the secret was.

We were in the tunnel of trees now and the headlights picked out the glistening leaves and the frilly flowers of the blackberry vines. Halfway through the tunnel lightning flashed again and again, and the trees stood out in a queer green radiance; above us, the storm broke.

At the same instant, something broke in Enrique, a suppressed fury that came out in measured deadly words, lighted with menace.

"You are not to see Meredith again. Since picking up strange men in cafes seems to come so easily to you, I can only presume that you were in the habit of doing this before you met me; but there will be none of that here."

I recoiled, not only shocked by an accusation that was brutal and unfair . . . and meant to be, I was sure . . . but by the intensity of his anger.

He was badly shaken, and I knew why. The likelihood of my accidentally running into another American in this tiny, isolated village had never occurred to him. It was a danger he had not considered.

Indeed, my meeting with Edward seemed almost providential, even to me.

Unnerved, knowing I was no match for Enrique, I defended myself as best I could, refusing to take this kind of battering lying down.

"If a friendly American stops to say 'hello' I answer him. I am not, however, in the habit of picking up strange men in cafes, unquote."

"Try telling that to the villagers after tonight's performance. And remember, whatever our private relationship may be, I will not be humiliated in front of my friends by having that relationship advertised. The surface appearances will be maintained, at least."

Ah, so that was another factor. Enrique's Spanish pride.

We had come out of the trees and turned up the drive. There was a threatening stillness in the car, broken only by the thud and splash of raindrops on the hood. The menacing words went on.

"Also remember this. Your friend Meredith will find Fuente land a dangerous place to be if he tries to come here. If he's foolish enough to get in touch with you, tell him that, for me."

With the whine of a rifle shot still echoing in my memory, I took this as no empty threat.

I shrank away from him. But I said in a light, hateful voice, "Pure melodrama. You're acting like a jealous husband in a silly play."

The minute the words were uttered, I regretted them. The phrase "jealous husband" had overtones of intimacy, and, even with Antonia making no plans for permanent departure, I still remained skittish around Enrique. I might be just enough like that other Lisa to be attractive to him.

Yes, the words had been a mistake. I felt a subtle change in atmosphere, an illusive new awareness overlaying the anger, like a flash of light seen from the corner of the eye.

It appeared and disappeared, leaving an intolerable excitement in the heightened air.

We had reached the garages and Enrique pressed the button that opened the electric doors; we passed through and the doors closed behind us, shutting out the world. Even the storm seemed far away, no more than the beat of a distant drum . . . or the sound of a pounding heart.

I sat silent and breathless. In the light from the dashboard I saw him turn toward me.

"No, I've never acted like a jealous husband," he answered in that soft voice that unnerved me so. "I've never acted like any kind of husband."

Then he added, "Until now."

Moving with deliberate slowness, he reached out and traced the fall of my hair down my cheek; and I was shocked to feel his touch leave a trail of fire across my skin. Still in that slow, strange way he slid his hand under my hair, caught the back of my neck in a ruthless grip, and pulling my face under his, clamped his hard, unrelenting lips against my own and kept them there.

The kiss was long and fiery, and dreadfully wrong; but I, shamefully, made no attempt to end it. Enrique was the first to hear the electric doors open again, the first to pull away. I straightened, then, and put my hands to my burning cheeks, just as the Mercedes carrying Alfredo and Nita whispered in beside us and came to a stop. Enrique reached to open the door on his side, but I sat still, feeling a creeping coldness at my heart.

Here was a man I feared, sometimes hated. I wasn't even sure he hadn't sent a cruel warning shot past me this morning. Added to all this, he was involved (in love?) with another woman.

And still, I had found his kiss an exciting thing. No wonder I felt sick with shame; and I knew that I would hate him afresh for this, perhaps because I hated myself so much at this moment.

Worse than the shame was the feeling of self-betrayal. I belonged to someone else, someone always close by now, a figure prowling the periphery of my consciousness, unable to reach me except across the treacherous terrain of my dreams. And I had removed myself still further from his reach by submitting to Enrique's expert, flaming kiss.

I made no move to get out of the car and Enrique leaned back through his window and flicked my cheek, in that way he had.

"Wake up, Lisa," he said. I could hear

laughter in his voice, and, infuriatingly, triumph.

I jerked away from his touch and reached for the door handle just as Nita came around to my side of the car. The sight of her indignant face, still wearing its chocolate mustache, steadied me.

"I'll walk in with you, *Tia* Lisa. Not with any uncles."

"I don't blame you," I agreed fervently.

Nita led me around the cars to a small door at the side of the garages. This door opened onto a wide, high-ceilinged breezeway that protected us from the lashing rain, and, half-running, half-walking, we went along it toward the house.

Enrique had stayed to say something to Alfredo, but was behind us now, catching up. Suddenly he reached us, leaned down and swooped Nita up in his arms.

"Uncles don't like being ignored," he said, his voice vibrant. "They like being friends with nieces."

My shame came burning back. In spite of Enrique's triumphant laughter in the garage, I'd begun to hope he'd been uncertain of my response, but I heard in his voice his awareness of my glowing fall.

It was at this moment that I began plotting my revenge.

"My husband," for all his strength, was a vulnerable man. His Achilles heel, his incredible pride, left him wide open. I knew just where to drive the arrow to make a deep and festering wound, a wound that would keep me safe from him forever, and more than make up for that searing kiss.

# Chapter 11

The breezeway led us to the lower floor of the house and a back door that gave access onto a long hallway. This hallway, judging from the delicious fragrances that reached us, went off in the direction toward the kitchen and servant quarters; the opposite direction, which we took, brought us into the dining room, and from there we went up the wrought-iron stairway to the second floor.

Enrique was still carrying Nita, and with the quick forgiveness of childhood, she had grabbed him about the neck and begun an enthusiastic conversation. I, making my secret plans, walked silently beside them.

When we reached the front of the house, we found the señorita in charge of Nita hovering at the bottom of the main staircase, anxious over the tardy homecoming; and Nita was allowed one sleepy kiss each for Enrique and me before she was hauled unceremoniously off to bed.

After she and her nurse had disappeared, Enrique and I stood still, caught again in that smothering light-streaked atmosphere that had surrounded us in the car. I was facing him, one hand on the stair railing. He reached out, in that slow way, placed his hand over mine and then pressed my hand hard against the polished railing. I seemed nailed into position and was unable to move until his voice released me.

"Dinner in an hour," he said roughly.

I pulled my hand away, and although my voice was tight and breathless, I said firmly, "I can't come down to dinner."

"Why not?"

"My head hurts," I answered, realizing that this was true.

He looked at me, started to say something, and changed his mind.

"All right, I'll send Feli with a tray."

I started up the stairs, determined to force him into the next move.

"Lisa."

I turned back.

"Shall I come up to you later?"

I let him wait. Then I smiled at him, a lying, radiant smile, filled with promise.

"Yes, come up to me later. I'll be waiting."

It hadn't been easy getting these words out, but they were said at last. I swung away from him and fled up the stairs.

When I reached my room I stepped inside and stood for a long time, listening to the pounding of my heart.

Later, sitting in front of the crackling fire someone had lighted for me, I reviewed my plans for Enrique's visit, only half-hearing the sounds around me, the brush of rain against the window panes, the squeaky laughter of a mouse behind the wainscoting.

Feli arrived, balancing a heavy tray with three covered silver dishes and a steaming pot of coffee on it.

She looked unlike herself tonight, and it wasn't until she had pulled up a small table and set down the tray that I realized what the difference was.

She wasn't wearing her uniform and the sight of her in her own clothes gave me a sad little shock. Her black dress was of some flimsy stuff that made her look slight and vulnerable, and her paper-thin black pumps seemed ready to come apart. Thrown across her shoulders was a cheap black coat that couldn't possibly protect her from the drive of the rain.

"I see you're going out tonight, Feli," I said.

"I'm going home, señora. Tomorrow is my day off and I'm allowed to leave the night before, if I finish with my work."

"Do you live in the village?"

"About halfway, señora. In one of the farmhouses on the way to the village."

In one of those dark, closed tenant farms, exuding age and poverty. My distress deepened and to add to my discomfort I realized that I had been speaking fluent Spanish.

So my careless tongue had led me on dangerous paths, in spite of my great care; but if Feli noticed she gave no sign. And I knew in that moment that she would never betray me. There had been a silent understanding between us from the first. Perhaps each of us subconsciously recognized and appreciated the other's struggle to keep afloat in hostile, frightening circumstances. Certainly, my problems were terrifying enough; and I guessed that Feli led a hard, lacerating kind of life just surviving the pull of her poverty-stricken family.

"It's still raining, you know. Will you be able to catch a ride?"

"Oh, no, I always walk. It isn't far."

I couldn't keep from glancing down at her shoes again, and following the direction of my gaze, she added earnestly, "Oh, not in these, señora. These are my best shoes, and I carry them in a sack when I go anywhere. For walking, I wear the shoes of my younger brother. His feet are now too large for them."

"Even so, you'll be cold in that coat, I think," I said, growing more troubled as I thought of the dark, lonely walk ahead of her.

Impulsively I reached out and picked up my coat from the back of a chair. "Please wear this. It's much warmer."

Feli turned bright hungry eyes toward the coat. "I couldn't do that, señora."

"Please, I insist."

I jumped to my feet, and in spite of much gentle protesting on Feli's part, I pulled off her coat and helped her into mine. I tied the belt around her and as I looped it in front, said, "You look wonderful."

This was true. All of Feli's sparkle had returned. We were like two delighted children playing dress-up.

"You won't need the coat, señora?"

"I have others for the rain."

I pushed her gently out the door, afraid she might change her mind; and with her "thank yous" still drifting back to me, I returned to my place before the fire.

Without interest, I lifted one of the silver covers on the dinner tray. Mountain trout, dressed with white grapes and wine sauce, but it was impossible for me to eat. Even though I felt better about Feli, there was still the showdown with Enrique to be faced. The time was growing short.

I drank a cup of coffee, forced down a few bites of *flan,* and rang for the maid. While I waited for her I felt a trickle of perspiration run down the back of my neck under my hair, and I got out my handkerchief and wiped it away.

After the maid had come and gone with the tray, I rose to my feet and closed the door. Then, carefully, I turned the key in the lock. After that I tested the door several times, and went about the room turning off lamps. Feeling light as thistledown, I returned to my chair and settled down in the firelight to wait.

As I waited, I felt a little smile curve my lips. I was considering, with satisfaction, the special welcome I had arranged for my proud Spaniard on our "bridal" night.

Enrique was not long in coming, and it sounded as though he took the stairs two at a time. Next came his swift triumphant footsteps crossing the *galería.* I traced his progress in my mind's eyes, seeing him as he would be, walking with that arrogant, inbred assurance that I knew so well. How certain he was!

He had reached the door now.

He turned the knob with a quick, exuberant twist. I watched, fascinated, as the knob was slowly released. Then it turned again, noiselessly, and came back more slowly still, to rest in its original position.

I shrank into my chair and sat listening to the silence beyond the door. And all the while, I thought again of how Enrique would look. The dark flush would be coming up in his face, an unbearably painful flush, I knew.

The stillness went on a little longer and then came a single word.

"Lisa?" The word was guarded and tentative.

At the sound of his voice I remembered, quite suddenly, that smouldering kiss in the dark of the car, and some abandoned part of me whispered: That was only a kiss, think of a night, an entire night alone with Enrique. How the darkness would shimmer, then! Open the door. Open the door before it is too late.

Dizzily, I listened to these treacherous, dreaming whispers, because I could not seem to silence them. But I did not move. I sat stubbornly on in my chair, scarcely breathing, letting the humiliating silence be my answer.

Vibrant seconds ticked by.

Then he was gone. For a long time afterward I could hear his unforgiving footsteps echoing back from the cold marble floors of the *galería*.

I remained in my chair, in the leaping firelight, until I was roused by a thumping on the stairs and the sound of voices. I got to my feet, opened the door a crack and looked out. The man-of-all-work, Juan, was depositing a set of the most beautiful luggage I'd ever seen at a door across the *galería*. It was a woman's luggage, midnight blue leather, fitted out with heavy brass locks and decorated with a single stripe of scarlet leather.

Without even guessing, I knew who owned that luggage. Antonia had returned, which was about as pleasant as having a black widow spider move in across the hall.

I closed my door, and crossed to my balcony where I threw open all the windows to the night. By leaning out the end window, I found I could see part of the drive at the front of the house, lighted now from the drawing room windows. There was little enough to see, but sounds carried in the wet air and it was pleasant to hear doors slam, a girl laughing somewhere, the clap of wings as a large bird rose in the dark.

Not caring that my hair grew slick and

wet, I continued to hang out the window, and after a while I saw Feli, on her way home at last, coming up the stone steps from the level of the dining room. She turned down the drive, walking between veils of rain, lifting in the wind.

She was oddly touching clumping along in her brother's heavy, too-big shoes, but I was comforted knowing that my coat enveloped her warmly.

I was so lonely that I longed to call out to her, but what was there to say? Regretfully, I watched her disappear into the tree shrouded darkness.

That night it was a long time before I slept and I awakened again toward morning, put on my robe and once more restlessly sought the open window at the end of my balcony. The rain had stopped and a cold moon lit the land and a high wind roared past the house. In the estuary, running water caught the light and marsh grasses turned silver.

I don't know how long I'd been on the balcony when I saw someone coming up the road beside the *ria,* toward the house.

A girl, slight, buffeted by the wind, hurrying. I watched, alert and wondering. Could Feli be returning for some reason? And at this unlikely hour?

No, not Feli. It was difficult to tell in the shifting moonlight, but this girl's raincoat seemed to be a leopard print one and her hair, disheveled and switching wildly about her face, was much shorter than Feli's.

Antonia.

A few minutes after I heard the front door opening and closing softly. Then I saw another figure, darker and more substantial, a man who wore a cap set jauntily on his head, and walked with lithe assurance. He kept to the shadows, moving swiftly when he hit the patches of light, pacing himself so that he was well behind Antonia. When he reached the steps that led to the dining room level, he turned and leapt lightly down them. Alfredo, returning to his room in the servants' quarters.

I stayed on the balcony, puzzling over what I had seen. Enrique's mistress meeting clandestinely with Alfredo? Was Antonia punishing Enrique for my unwanted presence? Had she seen Enrique at my door?

I cared nothing for what Antonia had seen or whom she met.

Why was it, then, that I felt disturbed, that I had the disagreeable feeling I had missed a step in the dark?

# Chapter 12

The next morning my breakfast tray was brought by a sour-faced maid who said, *"Buenos días,"* set the tray on a table on the balcony, and disappeared.

As I dressed, I thought the room too still without Feli to laugh and visit with; and there was a kind of unpleasant expectancy in the air, now that Antonia was back. My day wasn't improved by finding a note from Enrique on my tray, when I reached the balcony.

I recognized the distinctive black handwriting, although I had seen it only once before. I also recognized the imperative tone of the note. "You will appear at all midday and evening meals from here on in. Lunch at 2:00, dinner at 9:00." Nothing more. The hours were underlined and the note signed with a large "E."

I knew from the tone of this note that Enrique and I had completely regressed, just as I had meant for us to do. We were back in the days of our early relationship. Enrique was once more a dangerous stranger, but I did not regret my revenge.

I took a sip of tepid coffee and considered defying him in this matter of showing up at those difficult, interminable meals, but I knew I wouldn't do this. Defiance meant quarreling and contact. I wanted to keep as separate from him as possible.

That afternoon I asked if I might ride into the village to meet Nita again. I was hoping that I would see Edward. The more I thought about it, the more I felt that he understood how much I needed him, and the more certain I became that he would try to get in touch with me again.

When the Mercedes drove up to the front door where I stood waiting, I saw that Isidoro, the elderly gardener, was at the wheel. He explained to me in almost incomprehensible English that Alfredo was away on business for Don Enrique, for two days. I thanked him for this information in equally halting Spanish; then we each retreated to our separate sides of the language barrier and rode into town in dignified silence. I enjoyed the silence, highly pleased with the good news that Alfredo was to be away for even a short time. To be out of his watchful orbit was wonderful enough, but that was only the beginning.

Isidoro, far from spying on me, neglected his watchdog duties, and went off to visit his family the minute we reached town. This made an excellent set-up for a meeting, should Edward appear. My good luck didn't hold, however. I strolled around and around the square, keeping always in plain sight, watching hopefully.

Edward did not come. I sat down on a bench in the plaza to wait for Nita, preoccupied with my painful disappointment. This, in spite of the fact that the village was coming to life after siesta.

A narrow door opened on an upstairs balcony across the street, and I glanced up. An old woman, bent with arthritis, dressed in black, and with a black shawl over her head, appeared. She began to water the geraniums in the rusty tin cans that lined her balcony.

Watching idly, my attention was caught by a movement beyond the open door, by a face that I knew.

At the edge of the dimness, just back of the open doorway, Antonia stood looking down at me. I could not be mistaken. I had only a glimpse before she moved back into the sheltering darkness, but I was certain.

What was Antonia doing in such a place,

in one of the "dark houses?" And this house was a particularly disturbing one. I could almost smell the poverty behind the façade of peeling plaster and crumbling bricks.

Antonia must, of course, have friends in the village, but fitting the beautiful, elegant Antonia into this dying setting was difficult.

As I watched, the bent figure on the balcony paused in her watering, spun around, and stared directly at me. This stare was so inimical and malevolent that I turned sick with surprise. Pretending not to have seen, I looked down at my hands, and sat that way until Nita came a few moments later.

That evening Antonia did not appear for dinner, but Carlos was there, and for once I was glad to see him. He was a tedious man, much given to thrice-told-tales of his army life, particularly of the period he had served in Morocco. But anyone who filled up a chair was welcome as far as I was concerned. Considering the terms I was on with Enrique, I had no wish to sit down to a meal attended only by him, the grandmother, and me.

But even with Carlos' boring boom covering some of the more awkward moments, the dinner could hardly be considered a success. Enrique did not look at me, and every time the grandmother, with skillful politeness, tried to draw me into the conversation, my "husband," with equal skill and politeness, cut me out. I was reduced to complete silence, and retreating into my own thoughts, soon became absorbed in speculating about Antonia again.

I could not account for her presence in that house where I had seen her this afternoon. I raked through every possibility I could think of, becoming so preoccupied with the question that I startled myself and everyone else by asking abruptly, "Does Antonia spend much time in the village?"

"Antonia?" Enrique repeated, too astonished by this *non sequitor* to snub me. "As far as I know, she never goes there. Her friends are all in La Coruña, Barcelona, or Madrid. She is a city person."

"And she can afford to travel where she pleases," Carlos added sullenly.

I was to remember this remark later. At the time, I paid little attention.

So Antonia was not accustomed to making calls in the village. Yet she had done so today; and she obviously had at least one friend there. And a very strange friend she was.

Walking restlessly through the village on

138

the second day, I still saw no sign of Edward. Glancing down at my watch, I realized that it was a bare thirty minutes before Nita would be out of school and Isidoro returning to take us home.

I was standing in front of the *frutería*, disconsolately looking at a mound of apples, when Edward came. Suddenly he was there beside me, pretending to examine the apples, too, saying, "Well, Lisa?"

I turned and smiled at him, making no attempt to hide my joyful relief.

"I was afraid you wouldn't come."

"I said I would," he answered quietly.

That, I decided, summed him up pretty thoroughly. He had said he would help me and he had kept his word, automatically and without fuss. Here was a man I could count on. For the first time since I had awakened into my new life, I felt peaceful and protected.

"We can't talk here, you know," he said.

"No, we can't. Probably most of the shutters in the village are at half slant this instant. And Antonia, Enrique's cousin, has a ringside seat in a place above the bakery, when she's in town. There's simply no place to go."

"The church."

Of course. We strolled as casually as possible toward it, but even here there was one drawback. We might run into Father Fernando. Although I'd met him only that one time, on the day of my arrival, he'd seemed an interested and curious sort of man, especially where Americans were concerned. And Feli had told me he was extremely proud of the cathedral; he might invite us on a personally conducted tour .

We went up the steps to the lichen-covered face of the church and on through a great wooden door that looked as though it could stop a whole phalanx of warriors. As we entered the building the bells began to ring and each sweet, lingering note fell across us like a benediction.

Stepping inside, into the cool darkness, I looked for Father Fernando, but there was no sign of him. No one nearby at all, except a fat little priest with pink cheeks and a Friar Tuck hair-do, who passed us by with a murmured greeting and a beatific smile.

Edward guided me into one of the rear benches, and I allowed myself a swift glance about me. The church was Romanesque, with tier on tier of magnificent stone arches that rose fifty or sixty feet above the nave. At side altars, old women in black shawls were kneeling on the stone floor, their absorbed faces glowing in the lights of dozens of flickering candles. In the distance, at the end of the center aisle, was the main altar and on it was a silver statue of the Virgin Mary.

We were scarcely seated before Edward said in a low murmur, "Now tell me."

I told him everything from the beginning: about the car accident, about the hospital, my coming away with Enrique, about the papers. He sat with his elbows on his knees, his chin on his fists, listening to every word. He only interrupted me once, turning toward me curiously, "You mean you don't recognize anyone?"

"No one."

"It must be strange, not having any past."

" 'Haunted' is a better word. It frightens me sometimes to think of remembering again, of meeting up with the person I was. You see, I have no idea what I was like, whom I left behind by forgetting, what I might have been or done."

My voice must have risen a little because he said easily, "I shouldn't worry about all that now. The important thing is seeing how I can help you out of this situation that you seem to have got into."

I sat still, waiting, and he startled me by asking again, "Are you certain you recognize no one?"

"I've told you. No one."

"Quite a chance you took, coming away with Fuente."

"I was told that I had been identified as his wife. And at the time, it seemed unreasonable to think that Enrique would bring me here, if this weren't so. Now I know he had a most excellent reason. He needed me to sign the papers."

"If that's true, why don't you sign, and pull out? Let him have the money."

"Enrique has said he won't let me go under any circumstances. I think that even if I signed, he wouldn't dare, because I'm officially identified as Lisa Stephens. I suspect that a fortune is involved, and Enrique's taking no chances. If I got away I could cause a great deal of trouble . . . insist I'd signed under duress, for instance.

"And," I added, "although this may sound odd, I find it hard to sign those papers for another reason. I don't consider that money mine to give away. It belonged to a girl named Lisa Stephens, and as I've told you, I don't believe I'm that girl."

"Well, they can't make you sign. There would have to be witnesses, and they can't drag you in and use force in front of outsiders. And I must say they seem a pretty civilized lot for that sort of thing. After I saw you the other day I made inquiries . . ."

"Don't tell me. One of the oldest and finest families in Galicia. But I think they can make me sign finally, frighten me into it."

And then I told him about the rifle shot.

This caught his interest, but he persisted, "There's a good bit of hunting around here. Perhaps some farmer shot too close by mistake, then seeing you were all right, preferred to keep still. For which you can't blame him."

I saw that I was running up against my familiar problem of convincing the outside world that the Fuentes were not what they seemed, but charming conjurers.

"Whose side are you on?" I asked, feeling lost and angry.

He reached out and put his hand over mine, and warmth came flowing back into me.

"Yours," he said, with that attractive smile. "And it does sound as if things might be awry somewhere. Suppose I get you to Madrid, and we'll go to the American consul? Tell the consul what you've told me, and when Fuente shows up, let *him* do the explaining. It's about time, I think."

I turned to Edward in the shadows, excited, radiant with hope. "Yes, that's what I want. But how shall we manage it?"

He was looking at me but he didn't seem to be listening any longer.

"God, you're pretty," he said.

Abruptly, he faced toward the front of the church again, and a faint flush made his freckles stand out on his skin. I studied the hard, clean profile and the thick red eyelashes, much in evidence from this side view. Very nice, indeed, I thought. But it was the comfort, the peace he brought, that counted.

Still not looking at me, he went on, all business again. "We must plan. It's too late to do anything today. Come to the church tomorrow and wait inside. I'll be here about two o'clock and I'll drive up and honk. Come out casually, and we'll talk for a minute before you get in the car. I hope it'll look as though we're a couple of well-met compatriots, and that I'm giving you a short lift somewhere."

"And," he added fervently, "I also hope that damned watchdog who was hanging around the other day doesn't realize what's going on until we've gotten a good start. I don't want to lose time having to stop and brawl with him on the plains of Spain, in the rain."

"There's no problem there. Alfredo's doing his spying *in absentia* tomorrow. We'll be miles away before the other driver even knows we're gone. Isidoro visits his family when he comes to the village, and if he keeps an eye on me at all, it seems to be a most indifferent one. I'm sure Enrique hasn't the foggiest idea just how indifferent."

"Excellent. You're sure you can get here with no difficulty?"

"I'm sure. I come in every day now to meet Nita."

"O.K. I'll drive up in front of the church and honk three times, giving some time in between so we won't rouse the whole neighborhood. After the third honk, if you don't come out, I'll know something went wrong and that you couldn't get into town."

"Everything will go perfectly tomorrow. But I must go now," I answered, getting to my feet. Edward rose and followed, and as we left the church, I, glowing with gratitude, said, "You're a wonder to have worked this out. I could kiss you."

"I wish you would," he said quietly.

I could think of nothing to say to that.

He turned to leave and then turned back. "I have some advice for you. Until we get you out of town, trust no one." Then in a lighter tone, he added, "Beware of dark strangers."

"How about red-headed ones?" I asked,

surprised by this question that leaped out of nowhere.

He sent me a strange smile. "Safe as houses," he said.

# Chapter 13

The next afternoon, considerably before the appointed time, I was making my way up the cathedral steps. The day had run as smoothly as though it were set on wheels, everything fitting itself into place with my plans.

There was only one sad, dark spot in the scheme. Nita. I had begun by being enchanted by her, and ended by loving her. I knew that when she found I'd gone without a word, she'd feel betrayed.

There was no help for this. I had held myself in check all day, determined to give no sign to anyone that this day was to be different from any other for me. I must leave Nita without so much as the whisper of a good-bye.

As I reached the cathedral I saw that the door was partly open to the warmish, pleasant air, and I knew that there would be no difficulty in hearing Edward when he

147

honked the car horn. Everything was still falling into place.

I was too early and too excited; but I felt calmer in the cool stillness of the cathedral, and I saw with relief that I was quite alone.

I walked the length of one aisle, stopped at the central altar and studied it with pleasure . . . snowy altar cloth, magnificent brass candlesticks, Mary in her embroidered cloth-of-gold robes . . . all glowing in the jeweled light from a stained glass window.

I glanced down at my watch (still too early!) and moved on. Then I stopped again, staring in disbelief.

I saw a brass plate hanging on the wall, with the single word "Fuente" engraved on it. Under the plate was a small altar, set in a space about the size of a closet and closed off with a wrought-iron door that was locked.

So the lordly Fuentes, when they prayed, prayed alone, even in church.

"Incredible!" I said aloud.

The cherubic priest, whom Edward and I had seen the day before, appeared through a door at the back of the central altar. He saw me and came forward smiling.

"I am Father Domingo, Señora Fuente. You are here to see the cathedral? Splendid."

"Only for a few moments today, Father. I have a friend coming to pick me up soon."

"Another time, then," he said comfortably. "Now tell me, what is so 'incredible' about our church?"

Abashed to know that my exclamation had been overheard, I glanced up at the "Fuente" plaque.

"I was startled to find that the Fuentes have a separate altar, one just for themselves."

"That is not unusual, especially in the older Spanish churches. Distinguished families in a district often have private chapels. One sees many such chapels in all the larger churches. Our cathedral is small and we own one distinguished family, only. We must make the most of this."

His brown eyes glinted with humor; then he asked more soberly. "This arrangement of the separate altars is difficult for an American to accept?"

"A little, yes."

"I think I understand how it is with the Americans," he said, looking completely baffled. "You do not feel great reverence as the Spaniard does for these things ancient, ancient cathedrals and ancient families. Is it not so?"

It is not so that I feel great reverence for

your ancient families, particularly the Fuentes, I thought. But with a clear conscience I was able to tell him that I considered his cathedral very beautiful.

"Ah, yes." Then he went on in a deeply earnest voice, "But now that you are a Fuente, you must learn to feel differently about all things Spanish, I think. You must become a Fuente in essence as well as name."

Now that I was *not* to be a Fuente, I was able to answer cordially, "Yes, indeed, Father. I'm sure that's true."

Father Fernando had appeared less insular than this dear little rubber-ball of a priest. I was curious whether he was as dedicated and blindly loyal to the Fuentes as Father Domingo.

"Does Father Fernando share your reverence for your one 'ancient' family?" I asked curiously.

"Even more so. You see he is a distant connection of the Fuentes. And Spanish families are extremely clannish, all members intensely loyal to each other, no matter how remote the relationship."

While I was considering the implications of this statement, Father Domingo, gently explaining that he must be about his duties, took his departure. As I went back down the aisle, I was more grateful than ever that Edward had turned up to help me.

From the beginning I had considered that when I came to know the good fathers better, all else failing, I might go to them and explain my situation in the Fuente household. Now, thinking of the stone walls I'd have run into in that direction, I mentally wiped my brow.

Evidently, approaching either of the fathers for help would have been tantamount to asking Alfredo for a lift into Madrid.

I went back down the aisle, and settled myself on a bench near the cathedral entrance, where a wedge of mellowing sunlight fell through the half-open door. I looked anxiously at my watch once more, and saw I must wait at least another ten minutes for Edward. I closed my eyes and rested. In my excitement I had scarcely slept last night.

I was never to know later whether I dozed; but I must have, because my eyes leapt open with a frightened start, seeking my watch again. Edward had said two o'clock. Another five minutes, perhaps . . .

But it was at that instant that I heard a car horn honking.

I stumbled to my feet and made for the entrance, and it was a moment before I realized that there was a new dimness all about me, a dimness I did not understand until I reached the massive door and found it shut. With a rush of relief I saw, however, that it was not bolted.

I grabbed the carved-iron doorknob, turned it, and jerked with all my strength. The door did not open.

I pulled again, hard, and when the door refused to give, I felt perspiration dampen my face. I wiped my sleeve across my eyes, trying to think, to understand. The bolt was oiled and satin smooth, and had not been engaged. Hinges were blue-black with oil, and sunlight showed underneath the door, indicating a clearance of at least an inch. This great door had obviously swung easily inward for hundreds of years.

Another honk, tentative, louder.

The perspiration now clung to my face like a sheet of wet cellophane, and once again I brushed my arm across my eyes to clear my sight. Bracing my feet on the rough stones of the church floor, I took the doorknob in both hands, turned it carefully once more, and pulled with every ounce of strength I had. The door remained steadfast.

It was then, in despair, that I saw the key-hole. The door was locked. It had to be.

Chilling as though I had a fever, I turned and ran up the shadow-filled aisle, hunting for a rear exit.

Remembering the door behind the central altar, I tried that. It led into a large closet filled with vestments, hanging about the walls on hooks. I swung wildly about, flung myself out of the closet, and lost precious minutes searching. At last, I found a long stone passage where I saw light at the end, through a distant archway.

I began to run toward the light. Halfway down the hall, Father Domingo came backing out of a sidedoor that let onto the corridor. He was tugging at a sort of trolley cart affair that was loaded with stacks of heavy books. In this sideways position, Father Domingo, together with the cart, completely blocked the corridor.

"Father," I called wildly, still running, "could you make way, please?"

He looked up at me, startled, and then began pushing and pulling at the cart, attempting to turn it.

I reached him in a rush, and grabbing one side of the cart, tried to help jerk it around. Just as we'd managed to swing the cart and open a narrow passage for me, I heard it: one long, final blast of a car horn.

I let go of the cart and leaned against the wall, and felt tears standing in my eyes, burning like acid.

Father Domingo stared at me, his face puckered with distress.

"My dear, whatever can be the matter?"

"I was trying to find a way out of the cathedral," I answered, hoping he hadn't heard the humiliating sob that ended the sentence.

"But why didn't you go out the front door?"

"It was locked."

"Oh, no. Some dreadful mistake. In all the years I've been a priest here, the door of the cathedral has never even been bolted, certainly never locked."

I could not answer, and the acid tears spilled out of my eyes and ran down my cheeks.

"Señora . . . my dear señora Fuente, I shall go this minute and find Isidoro to take you home. He can return later for Nita."

I hardly heard him. I was listening to the noisy hum of a car engine, dying away in the distance.

# Chapter 14

Hearing breakfast being set up on the balcony next morning, I got out of bed and went to the French door. Yesterday's defeat had left me spent and discouraged, and I was hoping to see Feli. She wasn't there. It was that Maria, again.

After a cursory greeting, I started for my bath, thinking, as I recrossed the room, that I must have misunderstood about Feli's time off. And I'd overslept and missed Nita's occasional morning visit. Worst of all was the haunting memory of being locked in the cathedral, and the eerie fact that someone had known of my plan to go away with Edward yesterday and with consummate ease had thwarted this plan.

Once dressed, and on the balcony having breakfast, I saw that the weather had changed overnight and the day was clear and shining. My spirits rose a little.

Drinking my *café con leche*, I told myself

that my failure to meet Edward wasn't as disastrous as it seemed. It was a disappointing setback, and it meant starting all over. But Edward would return. We *would* get away together.

I had no idea about Edward's work schedule or when he might come again to the village. I would, of course, go in each day as usual, and wait.

I heard a small knock at my door, and to my delight saw Nita peering into the room. When she spotted me, she crossed to the balcony and said, "My dear, I've come to have breakfast with you."

"Delighted. Do pull up a chair and tell me why you're out of school."

She explained, while spreading marmalade half-an-inch thick on her bread, that she was out for the entire day. (No chance of my going into the village this afternoon, then.)

Her holiday was in celebration of some Saint's Day I had never heard of. There was to be a festival soon, too, which she planned to take me to, but today we would go fishing in the estuary.

This was just such a day as I needed, a day of forgetting. And I was sure it would be a day of relative freedom, too. I had noticed that when I was with Nita, the guards were called off. Enrique realized that I would never abandon Nita in some remote spot, even if it meant my getting away. For that reason she was an unaware, but effective guard.

Nita and I went off entirely on our own. No gardeners turned up pretending to dig nearby, there was no feeling of being watched from the long windows, and best of all, no Alfredo, although he had returned last night.

We roamed the hills around the house, fished in the estuary (without success), and ended up walking along the shore.

I cut all thought lines and surrendered myself to enjoying Nita and the glorious day, a day of warm winds and blown sunlight. Bees hummed in the wild rose hedges, and seagulls rode the wind above their racing shadows.

Once Nita, building a lopsided sand castle looked up at me and said, "*Tio* says your trunks have come from California and are in La Coruña now. Anna likes seeing trunks unpacked and seeing American clothes."

"I'll make sure she's notified the minute the trunks arrive," I answered, smiling. I had become accustomed to speaking to Nita through her alter ego.

I looked out at the glimmering sea,

thinking about the clothes arriving from California. I had come to feel a strong affinity with Lisa Stephens, this girl I'd never known, and I thought her clothes might tell me something about her. I felt that she would not have minded my going through her things in my effort to discover her.

Remembering my order from Enrique to appear at all meals, and still wary of stirring up any fresh conflict with him, I saw to it that Nita and I were back well before lunch time. We arrived home disheveled, and much pleased with ourselves, and before separating arranged a date for the afternoon.

I went to my room and washed my hands, but made no further attempt at repairing the ravages of my outing. I disliked being ordered to lunch, and I took my dislike out in childlike defiance, arriving sans lipstick, flaunting my windblown hair.

The instant I entered the drawing room and saw Antonia standing next to Enrique, I realized I had put myself at an unnecessary disadvantage and I regretted what I had done.

Antonia was wearing a sleeveless pink linen that showed off her lovely arms and fell in a pale perfect line. Not a ghost of a wrinkle anywhere and that heavy auburn hair alight in the sun.

I tilted my chin a little higher, crossed the room and shook hands with her. Then I said I was delighted she had returned, which wasn't true.

"How are you?" Antonia asked. I realized then that she had never smiled at me or called me by name. "Is your health improving?"

"My health is excellent," I replied, flushing hotly.

The entire family was assembled at this end of the room, with Father Fernando there, too. I had reached Enrique now and everyone seemed to be watching us. He leaned over and kissed my cheek. The kiss was light and cold. I swung away from him, spoke to Carlos in passing, and went to pay my respects to the grandmother.

"Did you and Nita enjoy your morning at the seashore?" she asked, with her thin smile.

"Yes, indeed," I answered, startled.

How had the grandmother known about my whereabouts this morning? Had she sent Alfredo to spy on Nita and me, after all? Had he stood quietly behind some tree or watched us from a secret ridge?

Disturbed, I went to a couch and sat down alone. Father Fernando followed, bringing me a glass of sherry.

"Thank you, Father."

He inclined his head and sipped his sherry in silence. At last he spoke, his voice troubled. "I regret what happened to you in the cathedral yesterday. Father Domingo told me of it. You said the main door had closed and you couldn't get out, I believe. I have never known it to do so before, but perhaps it did swing to. You should, however, have been able to open it. It moves easily on its hinges."

"I realize that the door swings easily, Father. But it wasn't a question of its being closed. The door was locked. I tried again and again to pull it free."

Father Fernando looked away for a moment, but not before I had seen the disbelief in his eyes.

"As I say, it is possible that the door was momentarily closed. Locked, never."

"It has a keyhole," I persisted.

"A keyhole, yes. Our cathedral is very old and perhaps at some point in its history it was necessary to lock this door. But in the years since the church has been in my care, there has been no such need. The door stands open even through the night."

I saw I was not helping my cause by insisting that the door had been locked. It was obvious that Father Fernando did not believe me, and I thought it likely that the villagers were already beginning to equate my amnesia with mental instability. I did not want Father Fernando and Father Domingo to start thinking along such lines.

"I'm sure I must have been mistaken about the door, Father."

"It's not important. It's just that I wanted you to know that you must never be frightened in our church. It is, after all, a sanctuary. As you learned when Father Domingo led you out, the cathedral has many doors, and all of them, in the usual way of things, wide open."

Still, I couldn't resist asking, "And when Father Domingo went back to the front door, was it closed?"

"No. The door was open and the key was hanging on its brass hook, at the side of the altar, as always. Father Domingo doubts that such an ancient key would work in the lock, had someone tried to use it. And, of course, there seems to be no reason why anyone should."

"None at all," I said, staring blindly down into my glass.

On the third morning after Feli's leaving I asked Maria about her. Was she ill?

"Perhaps," Maria answered indifferently.

161

Or perhaps there had been some other difficulty. Who was to say? Feli came from a large family with many problems and was often delayed several days in getting back to her job.

Feeling troubled, I asked Nita later if Feli had yet returned and learned that she had not. No one seemed to be taking any interest in the matter except me, and I was relieved to hear that when she still hadn't shown up in the late afternoon, the grandmother sent Alfredo to inquire about her.

That was when it was discovered that she had never reached home at all.

Her worried family explained that when she hadn't come home the evening she was expected, they had assumed that her free day was switched to another time, as often happened. They felt no alarm, and it hadn't occurred to them to check, since her schedule was flexible.

At that time she had been missing three full days.

The Guardia Civil was notified and a thorough search of the area begun, but even as the search progressed the villagers and the Fuentes seemed more mystified than suspicious of any really terrible happening. Feli was among people she had known all her life. Who would harm her?

Still, my anxiety increased with every passing hour; but perhaps that was because my fear for Feli knew another dimension, one that I couldn't bear to face. Not until there was proof that harm had come to her.

The search continued. It was thought that she had met with an accident. A tumble into a deep ditch, perhaps; a branch falling and dazing her so that she had crawled off the highway and lost consciousness. She could still be found in time to save her. This accident theory had to be discarded almost immediately. Every yard of the land between the Fuentes and Feli's house was soon gone over several times. She wasn't there.

A member of the Guardia Civil came to talk with Enrique.

I, sitting tautly on one of the red velvet couches in the drawing room, strained to hear what was being said.

It was more a friendly conference than an inquiry. The young policeman had been born in the area and he and Enrique had known each other as school boys. He was thorough and persistent in his questioning, but his flashing smile was deferential.

Even had he been a stranger, I was sure the friendly deference would have been there. After all, Enrique, in his position . . .

what possible connection could he have with the disappearance of a minor member of his staff, one whom he hardly knew?

Foul play was not discussed. Certainly there was no indication of this, no signs of a struggle, no straying bits of clothing.

It was known, the young officer explained, that Feli had two rather erratic friends who had run off to work in Madrid. Did Don Enrique think it likely that Feli had joined them? Enrique replied that he supposed this was possible. It was true that Feli came from a large, impoverished family, and since her father had been ailing during the last year, she had been the main financial support of this family.

Enrique, shrugging, said it might be that she had grown tired of her excessive responsibilities and had gone to Madrid. He really couldn't say.

The young man thanked him and said they were looking into the possibility of strange cars in the area that evening to determine whether she might have caught a ride from the village. She had not gone by bus, of course, because as Señor Fuente well knew, the bus only ran once a week and the day had been wrong for that. The Guardia Civil was also making efforts to trace Feli's friends in Madrid.

Enrique wished him luck, asked to be informed of any further developments, and walked him out to the end of the drive.

After they had gone, I sat considering the possibility of Feli's being safe in Madrid with her friends, trying to believe this, because I needed to. But I found it difficult to accept the fact that she had run away and left her family to fend for themselves, and while it was a small thing, I didn't think she would have gone off wearing my expensive coat.

Still there was nothing I could do but wait, refusing to listen to the whisperings of a new kind of fear in the corners of my mind.

# Chapter 15

Saturday afternoon, two days later, I had my usual date with Nita, and it was just past the siesta when I left my room to go down for her. Carlos, with what seemed oddly coincidental timing, stepped out into the *galería* at the exact moment as I.

"Ah, my dear, are you off for a ramble with Nita on this beautiful afternoon?"

"Yes," I answered, moving swiftly toward the stairs.

I wasn't quick enough. Although he was a heavy man, he was beside me in an instant, and before I knew what was happening, he had stepped around in front of me and trapped me at the head of the stairs.

His smile remained avuncular but his eyes roamed my face, and his nearness disconcerted me, particularly at this time of day when the house was so still as to seem deserted. He was facing me, and his breath stirred the hair falling forward against my cheek.

"You mustn't let that little rascal of a Nita monopolize your time this way. The rest of us see too little of you."

"I spend my time with her by my own choice," I said coldly.

"Even so, I'm sure we'd like to see more of our new relative," he went on in a low voice, and he reached out and gave my cheek a cruel pinch. "I know I would."

"Well, I'm afraid it will have to be another time," I answered, as a shudder of revulsion swept through me. "And now if you'll let me pass, please. Nita will be up from her nap and expecting me."

"Oh, sorry. I didn't realize I was blocking your way . . ." his tone was jovial, and he stepped aside. Not far enough aside, it seemed, and his arm brushed lingeringly against mine in passing.

I went down the stairs, cold with disgust, thinking how expert he was. He had done nothing I could pinpoint, even if I could have gone to Enrique. But threat was implicit in the whole performance. What an odious man to be cooped up in a house with.

I reached the second floor with relief and hurried off to the rooms beyond the library that Nita shared with her señorita.

The señorita was still in her own room, but Nita, who was already dressed, assured me that there wasn't a moment to lose; and we were on our way promptly, walking down the road past the estuary to a sun-bright sea. As we went I almost forgot Carlos, but not quite.

Nita and I spent another blissful afternoon together, but it was marred at the end by the sight of Alfredo walking the hills in the distance with a shotgun in the crook of his arm.

Something about the easy way he carried the gun shocked me; and Nita, unfortunately, had seen him, too.

"What is Alfredo doing?"

"Hunting," Nita answered, and she closed one eye, and squinting with the other, looked with interest at her tennis shoes.

"What does he hunt?"

"Rabbits." After a pause, she added, "Even baby ones. He likes to kill things."

Then she gave a little gasping hiccough.

That evening, in order to be better prepared to deal with Antonia . . . and also to distract myself from crowding painful thoughts . . . I took time over my dressing, putting on the dress that I thought the prettiest of the ones Enrique had bought me.

It was a Thai silk caftan. Its stripes were a gradation of muted blues, and it shimmered and floated when I walked. With it I decided to wear the diamond and aquamarine pin that Enrique had told me was my wedding present. I did not believe this. It seemed more likely that a true Fuente bride would have been given a family piece.

This was a new and dazzling thing. Just such a gift as Enrique might have purchased for Antonia. I thought it possible that in his anxiety to convince me I was his bride, and having the pin laid by, he had taken it out and given it to me, on impulse.

Certainly it had been purchased after the accident. Had it been bought before the wedding, it would have been destroyed in the crash, along with everything else.

Perhaps Enrique had told Antonia about the pin, explaining how it had ended up in my possession. In case this might be so, I fastened it to the caftan with malicious satisfaction.

From the minute we entered the dining room, Antonia's attention focused on the pin like a laser beam. She turned quieter and sulkier as we dined, and I allowed myself a triumphant inward laugh.

Carlos also seemed uncommonly interested in the pin and studied it through narrowed, resentful eyes. The aquamarine, glowing deep blue in its rim of fiery diamonds, must appear an alarmingly expensive piece of jewelry, even to the uninitiated.

I remembered one evening at dinner when Carlos had spoken enviously of Antonia's money and freedom to travel, and I guessed that although he must have some sort of retirement from the army, he was essentially Enrique's pensioner, and a dissatisfied one at that. Evidently Carlos was taking a dim, petulant view of what he considered gross extravagance on the part of his benefactor.

Even Enrique reacted peculiarly to his "wedding gift." He took one look at the aquamarine and never looked back at it again. When he was compelled to direct conversation my way, he stared steadily past my right cheek.

Another small triumph, but it didn't last long.

The conversation soon turned to guarded speculation about Feli's whereabouts, and the evening was ruined for me. The others grew disturbed, too. Although everyone agreed that Feli must have run away, her disappearance was beginning to cast a long shadow.

That night, when I slept, I dreamed again of someone walking away from me in the rain, but this time it wasn't the man I'd always seen before. It was Feli . . . Feli, with the same dark hair as mine, going down the driveway in my red coat, clearly visible to anyone who might have been watching from the windows of the house.

I awakened, drenched in perspiration, my eyes wide with terror in the darkness.

The next morning I had a low-grade but persistent headache. As this was Sunday, Nita and I had plans for an excursion after she returned from church. I dressed dully, and was finishing a token breakfast when she showed up in my room. She reminded me that we were to go into the higher hills back of the house and climb on rocks. There was a hole in one of these hills, with a cave under it, she explained. "It's called the 'River Cave.'"

"I know all about that cave."

"We'll have to be careful not to fall in it."

"We'll be careful," I assured her grimly. "About everything."

"Could we find the path that leads down to the cave and go look inside it?"

"We'll see," I answered lightly. "Someday, perhaps."

This was a promise that I had no plan of keeping. The idea of the cave, with its dark, icy river, repelled me.

As we started out I noticed that the air had lost its clarity and the wind was rain-scented. As Nita and I went out the back of the house and down toward the meadow, I saw sheets spread out on the grassy knolls to dry. Perfect timing, I thought wryly. Then I realized that Nita and I, in our light sweaters might get wet ourselves, but I decided finally that we could make it up to the hills and back before the rain began.

As it turned out, we never got past the *hórreos*. I glanced over at them as we went by, thinking again how like sepulchers they were, and at the same time I noticed that the door of the nearest one was open. I was sure this wasn't a good idea. If there were grain inside, it would become damp. I paused and stood looking at the *hórreo*, considering whether I should call someone to set things straight.

And that was when I saw it . . . a single human finger curled around the edge of the open door.

# Chapter 16

I neither moved nor made a sound. I lowered my eyes and stared at the earth, and then I looked again.

Nothing had changed, the finger was still there. I locked my teeth against a scream. Nita must not know.

She had gone on ahead a few yards and I called to her in a muffled voice. She turned back and stood looking at me; and I knew that the horror that held me was like an evil stench, communicating itself.

"We must return to the house. I'm not feeling well."

Still she didn't speak, but reached out and grabbed my hand and clung to it as we made our way back.

When we reached the house again and were inside in the main hallway, I leaned down to speak, trying to make my voice normal, but it came out in a raw terrible whisper.

"Go find your señorita," I said.

She reached up, caught me by the neck, and held on tightly for an instant. Then she turned and ran as hard as she could go toward her room.

I walked on down the hall. When I came to the drawing room, I saw through the open door that there was a maid there.

I stopped and leaned against the doorjamb and she glanced up; then giving me a startled look, she said, "Señora, you look ill."

"Go and call the Guardia Civil," I said. "Tell them there's a body in one of the *hórreos*."

I turned away, went up the stairs and into my room. There I threw myself face down on the bed, and wept.

Feli had not gone to Madrid, as I had known all along. She had been murdered, wearing my red coat. I kept remembering how I had urged the coat on her. I was thinking, too, that if I had called out that night, the murderer might have been thrown off in his plans, might have hesitated just long enough for Feli to be saved. Regret and guilt swept through me, searing, destroying as they went.

By evening I had such a racking headache that I lay very still, not daring to turn my head, and, although I couldn't remember when this happened, I found I had been undressed and put between cool sheets.

People came and went in the room, but there seemed to be a mist around my bed and I had difficulty identifying them. I thought I saw Enrique there, but I couldn't be sure, because I kept getting this illness confused with the illness after the accident. The grandmother, too, seemed to be in the room, drifting through the air.

When she and Enrique came too close I felt alarmed, so I lay stiller yet and gave no sign.

At last a doctor came and took my pulse and spoke to me through the mist. I felt peaceful with him there and when he mixed something in a glass and told me to drink it, I obeyed.

After that the headache lessened and I slept.

When I awakened, I turned my head cautiously and found it no longer hurt, and looking out from under the edge of the compress that covered my eyes I could see sunlight streaming in on the bed and I guessed that it was midmorning. I had slept well, then, all night.

I lifted the compress and looked about me, and decided that in spite of the sunlight it must be cold outside. All the windows were closed and the wind was singing a sad song in the trees. Over before the fire, a plump partridge of a nurse sat in a chair reading a lurid looking Spanish paperback.

I studied her, knowing what I had to ask. I decided that she must speak some English, that it would be necessary for her to do so, as a nurse.

I took a long breath and said quickly, "It was Feli . . . in the *hórreo,* wasn't it?"

She threw the paperback straight into the air, and blushing, stumbled to her feet.

"Forgive me, señora," she replied in accented but clear English. "I thought you were not yet awake."

"Was it Feli?"

"I'm not supposed to talk to you about that matter, señora."

No, I imagine not. But she *must* talk. There was something I had to be certain of.

I saw that the nurse was young and appeared out of her depth in this situation, and I was sure she was accustomed to obeying commands.

"Answer me, please," I insisted.

"Yes — she — it was Feli."

"Was she shot?"

The nurse twisted her fingers together. "No, señora. She was struck from behind with a large stone."

"Was she wearing a red coat when she was struck?"

"Yes, señora."

A long shudder shook me and I put the compress back over my eyes.

Tears kept welling up and soaking into the cloth, but I knew I couldn't allow the luxury of tears, either for Feli or myself. Feli was gone, murdered in my stead. But why? The papers were still unsigned, yet someone wanted me dead.

The murderer, seeing Feli walk off toward the avenue of trees and thinking it was I, must have been waiting for just such a moment, and had acted quickly . . . someone, then, who made a practice of watching all my moments, looking for his chance, someone who could keep careful track of me because he was close at hand.

A member of this household, I thought, my body chilling and burning at the same time. And his mission was still unaccomplished. He walked these halls and slept not far away at night. Did he smile in his sleep, not minding that he had mistaken Feli for me, dreaming his terrible dreams?

I must get out of this place. Now. I couldn't wait for Edward to come to me; I must go to him in Lugo.

I hadn't been able to discover how far it

was to Lugo, but I had learned from Feli that there was only one hotel there. There would be no difficulty in locating Edward once I got in town.

But I couldn't simply strike out across the country walking, looking for Lugo. Alfredo or Enrique, or the Guardia Civil, could run me to earth in thirty minutes. No, I must take the bus; but it only ran on Fridays, four days from now.

I would have to get away by night, as I had originally planned. I felt dizzy at the thought of that lonely night walk — along the same route Feli had taken. But there was no other way to escape this house; and there was this difference: My departure would be secret, and I would be watching every instant, and I knew hiding places along the way.

I must remember to allow time, not only to get to the village, but to get through it and find a place to conceal myself through the next morning. I must be waiting a good distance away, on the far side, because the bus's arrival and departure were events in the village and attended by half the populace.

Even so, I still stood a good chance of being recognized by some of the passengers. Upon their return they would undoubtedly report that I had been seen hailing and boarding the bus. By the time this word got to Enrique, I hoped to have reached Lugo and Edward.

Trying not to think of the flaws in this scheme, I went on planning. I had been hoarding most of the *peseta* notes that I found in my purse, later putting them in an envelope and pinning them inside my slip, so that I always had my money with me. All this had been made possible because of Nita, who, generous to a fault, invariably spent her last *peseta* treating me.

It was a sad little stockpile and I wasn't sure it would cover the price of a bus ticket, plus money for food, and perhaps an overnight stay.

No, it wasn't enough money, but I would steal more from Enrique. He must keep running funds for the household on hand, either in his room or in the desk in the library.

I would have been riffling through his desks in any case, I thought coldly. This was the only way I could get hold of my passport. I had no compunction about taking anything I needed from Enrique, and the minute I could get out of bed I would begin by searching his bedroom during the siesta time, when he was always out of the house.

Comforted now that I was taking action, I slept again.

When I awakened I felt stronger. I lifted the cloth from my eyes and saw, with gratitude, that the nurse was still there, back in her chair by the fire. I hoped that I could keep her near me for the rest of my stay in this frightening house. She was my one contact with the outside world.

"I seemed to have dropped off," I said, smiling at her. "How long have I slept, please?"

The nurse got quickly to her feet when I spoke. "Since you were first ill, señora?"

"Yes."

"Three days."

Another shock. I had thought it was only yesterday that I had found Feli. Had I been asleep all that time? Or had I had another lapse and forgotten again? Newly disturbed I lay struggling to piece the last three days together.

*You can't force yourself to remember, Dr. Markam had warned me. The amnesia victim has an inhibition against recall. The important thing, if you have a relapse, is not to grow alarmed. Emotional upsets tend to make any kind of amnesia more destructive, to set back the recovery timetable.*

I couldn't afford setbacks or delays of any

kind. I knew now that every minute spent in this house was a dangerous one, whether the papers were signed or not. I made a conscious effort to calm my thoughts, to slow the racing beat of my heart.

One good thing, I thought wryly, since this was Wednesday, not Monday, it was two days, not four, until the bus ran.

That evening Enrique and Nita and Anna came to call. I didn't like having Enrique so near; and even with the nurse there, I was glad for Nita, whose presence threw an automatic circle of safety around me.

Nita approached my bed and said in a piercing whisper, "I've got splendid news for you *Tia* Lisa."

"I could use a little."

She leaned forward, and watching me with shining eyes, wiggled her front tooth. "My tooth is loose."

"No! I'm astounded."

"What's this 'astounded'?" she asked, looking faintly disappointed.

"Never mind. Just bear in mind that I'm an expert at pulling teeth, when they're very loose. I use American methods, of course."

"Well, bless my buttons, but that's an excellent bit of luck."

And I, for the first time in days, laughed aloud.

Enrique, who was standing with one arm on the mantel, staring down into the fire, seemed lost in his own preoccupations and didn't respond or smile. His face in repose looked haggard.

No wonder. Housing a murderer was quite a responsibility. Or being one.

I didn't realize that I had been staring at him, and he, looking up and catching my eye, said abruptly, "I think we should be going now, Nita."

"Very well," Nita answered, hauling Anna up off the floor by the hair and bringing her around and stretching her out on the bed beside me.

Then she came back around the bed and kissed me on the cheek, a kiss as light as the touch of a butterfly's wings.

"Anna will take care of you, *Tia* Lisa. You needn't be frightened any more."

After they had gone, I thought: No word of what had happened to Feli would have been allowed to filter down to Nita, but with the strange omniscience of childhood she had caught the reverberations of fear and death.

The next morning I awakened feeling

more refreshed, more determined. I had breakfast with my nurse, whose name was Paca. Quizzing her gently, I discovered that she had been installed in the Fuente household at the insistence of the doctor, not Enrique.

Paca proved to be shy, tractable, and placid, all characteristics that aided and abetted me in my afternoon's plan. At three o'clock sharp, Paca settled herself on the cot that had been installed in my room for her, closed her eyes, and fell asleep instantly. Here was a woman who took her siesta seriously, but I couldn't be sure of the rest of the household, and I waited for another thirty minutes, until the house was wrapped in stillness.

Going next door, to Enrique's room and entering, was uncomfortable work, and I left the door wide open behind me. I thought I could hear anyone coming up the stairs. Certainly I would know if someone crossed the marble floor of the *galería*, where footsteps echoed.

I had never been in Enrique's room before and I looked about me curiously.

This room was the duplicate of mine in plan and size, the walls white, the beams dark. There were no rugs, only highly polished parquet floors, and the bed was covered with a simple handwoven spread in red cotton. There were two oversized lounge chairs, one on either side of the fireplace, a fruitwood chest of drawers, and a desk, a beautiful old English one.

I walked over to the desk, sat down nervously in front of it, pulled at the narrow top drawer. It stuck a little and as I worked at it, slowly and in dead silence, I felt a pulse begin to beat heavily at one temple.

I kept at my search and as the drawer came open I saw that I had been right about the money. There was quite a lot of it, thrown carelessly in the corner of the drawer. I took three one-hundred-*peseta* notes, and longed to take more, but I didn't dare.

I went through three more drawers; there was no sign of the passport. Spying is hot work, and I opened the last drawer with sweaty fingers. I lifted out papers and laid them noiselessly on the desk. No passport among them. But I found something else, a puzzling thing, and even before I began to understand, I felt alarmed.

It was a paper folder with the single word "Lisa" on the outside cover. Inside there was a complete history of my illness. There were letters to the doctors in San Francisco and their corresponding replies, in English, and a résumé of my illness, signed by the hospital doctors, also in English.

There was a detailed progress report in Spanish, describing the frequency of my headaches and their intensity, as surmised by the writer, and a description of my general behavior. In this behavioral description, it was pointed out that I was easily frightened, that I seemed to feel the entire family was against me. It went on to say that I had had a severe setback recently over the death of a maid, of whom I was fond, and that it was possible I had had a fresh memory lapse.

There was more, but I didn't read it. I didn't need to, because I no longer found this file puzzling.

I found it the most terrifying document I had ever run across; and struggling against tears and nausea, I folded my arms on the desk, put my head down, and tried to think.

The fact that Enrique had kept a file on me at all was shocking enough. The progress report in Spanish, obviously meant for Spanish doctors, told the tale, and I knew exactly what it was.

It was a meticulously kept record that would be used, I was sure, to prove me mentally incompetent. It appeared complete, and totally damaging. No wonder there had been no further effort to make me sign the papers. There was no need. Enrique had found an easier and less dangerous way to get the money he needed.

But the fact remained that Feli had been murdered in my stead. Did that mean that there was someone else, someone working quite separately from Enrique, who wanted me dead . . . someone whose vicious reason I couldn't even guess at?

If this were so, then there were two stalkers in the shadows, each of them in his separate way, determined to destroy me.

# Chapter 17

That evening Enrique came to my room once more, accompanied by Nita.

I had wished after what I had learned this afternoon that I might never lay eyes on him again; but since this was impossible, I had worked out my own special plan for facing him during the next two days.

"I'm glad to see you're up and about, Lisa," he said formally. "Perhaps, since you are, you'd like a breath of air and a run into the village. Nita and I are going in. There's a religious procession, and people from the farms and all the neighboring villages come to town."

"It's very noisy," Nita offered hopefully.

"Sounds nice," I answered, and, although I could feel two spots of color burning my cheeks as I looked at Enrique, I smiled my best smile and said quickly, "Yes, I'll go. I'd love an evening out."

The cordial smile seemed to rattle

Enrique, and I was pleased. Feeling safe and comfortable with Nita along, I realized that this outing suited me perfectly. I wanted to appear in public, enjoying a happy, normal evening with my family, because my plan now was to confuse and confound. I had been too open, too quick to show my feelings and admit my headaches. I should have dissembled, pretending to be well at all times, returning lying responses that couldn't be pinned down.

I was certain that even Enrique, with all his influence, could not bring off his scheme without good hard facts and witnesses outside the family. And while I was trying to keep faith with my escape plan and believe in it, I couldn't be sure that it would succeed. In any case, it would do no harm to throw out as baffling a smoke screen as possible.

I grabbed a coat and said, "Race you to the car," to Nita.

She caught fire from my mood and we went clattering down the stairs and through the hall, out into a scented dusk. The air was filled with sleepy bird calls, and the moon, just rising, threw a strange golden glow over the land.

The strangeness and the glow went on and were part of the evening. Even Enrique, once we were on our way, couldn't seem to hold out against the ridiculous chatter and flow of laughter, and began to thaw visibly. And I, pretending exuberance, had begun to feel exuberant. Perhaps part of this was the beautiful night, the holiday feeling, the excitement in the air as we drove into the village.

The place was jammed, people everywhere in the streets, and spilling off the sidewalks. There was no place to park around the square, so that we were forced to drive on through and out the other side in order to find a parking place. Enrique, as was his practice, tossed the keys carelessly on the floor of the car, under the seat. He and Alfredo and Pepe, the manager of the salt operation, all did this, even with the jeep, because they were constantly exchanging cars, often arranging the exchange by phone, and they found this easier than carrying dozens of keys.

Besides, as Enrique had arrogantly explained when I asked him about it, people didn't steal cars in the country, particularly the Fuente cars which were known throughout the district.

No, indeed, not the Fuente cars, I thought, freshly annoyed as we made our way back to the square. Such insolence wasn't to be thought of!

But I forgot my annoyance when we got back into the excitement of the crowded streets. The sidewalk cafe was doing a roaring business and we had to wait some time for a table. While we were waiting we saw Alfredo a short distance away, walking with a pretty, fragile-looking girl.

When Nita dropped back briefly to visit with a friend, I asked, "Who's the girl with Alfredo?"

"His *novia*. The girl he's engaged to."

"Why that miserable cheat . . ." The words were out before I could stop them.

Enrique turned and looked directly at me. There was a curious stillness in his face.

"Why do you say that?"

"No reason . . . I don't like Alfredo, that's all . . ."

What did I care for the Alfredo-Antonia-Enrique triangle? Even so, it seemed small-minded and spiteful to be the tale bearer.

"You had a reason," Enrique replied, still in that quiet, listening sort of way. "I want to know what it was."

"I saw him and Antonia coming home together late one night . . . very late." Then getting into the spirit of the thing, I added airily, "It was only two a.m., actually. I'm sure it was all quite innocent."

"No doubt," Enrique answered, his face hard and closed.

Then Nita returned, we found a table, and I forgot them all. Enrique brought me a sherry, which promptly went to my head; and I settled down to having a wonderful time, snatching joyfully at this brief respite from my troubles. It was like a gift from the Galician night.

By the time I had finished my sherry the procession had begun to form, far up on a hill, and the flames of the torches of the distant marchers leaped and danced in the wind, burning clear and bright against the dark sky.

We got to our feet and strolled through the jostling crowd; and Enrique, after several broad hints from Nita, bought packages of toasted almonds from the almond vendor, for her and me.

We laughed and nibbled as we walked, listening to the high drumming chant of the marchers, who were quite close now. Enrique directed us toward a white wall a little distance away. He thought we'd be out of the way of the procession there, but still able to see.

The crowd had grown more concentrated, thickening imperceptibly and becoming unwieldy, turning the cool air warm with its collective breath. At the same time the street was inundated with the marchers, and I stared at them, fascinated and repelled.

They wore black robes that furled and unfurled in the leaping light of the torches; and their eyes glittered through the narrow slits in the black cloth that masked their faces. Their tall, conical hats were like pointed black shadows on their heads, and they looked as though they belonged in another time — as though they had come swaying up dark, wet steps from dungeons of the Inquisition.

"Lisa! Over here."

It was Enrique and I realized that as I'd lingered, the crowd had separated me from him and Nita. Before I could answer, the procession drove a wider wedge between us and I was thrust back against the white wall.

The crowd was an inert, smothering thing, pressing steadily harder. Then a large man backed directly into me and cut off most of the air, and I grew panicky and yelled, "*¡Por favor, señores!*"

No one paid the slightest attention, but two teen-age boys sitting on the wall above me looked down and called out in delighted voices, "Have no concern, señorita. Free your arms and reach up to us. The wall is low; we'll pull you up."

But getting my arms free and raised above my head took some doing, and I was making no headway at all until one of the young Spaniards put a large foot into the back of the man who had pinned me to the wall and pushed until I got maneuvering room. Then the two of them reached down for me and pulled me up and deposited me with a teeth-jarring jolt on the wall between them.

I took a long breath of fresh air and looked across the top of the crowd for Nita and Enrique. They were a good distance away and cut off from me by the procession, but Nita saw me and waved. Enrique stood watching me with a hard little frown deepening between his eyes.

Meanwhile, my rescuers were close at hand and regarding me as though I were some large, delicious fish they'd just pulled out of the sea. I would have found this amusing at another time, but an idea, still half-formed but there, was beginning to burn in my brain like a hot coin; and all I wanted at the moment was to be free of my interested young friends, and alone on the wall.

"Thank you, señores," I said politely. "My husband, Enrique Fuente, will want to thank you, too, so if you could come with me to meet him after the procession is over . . ."

That did it. My companions were definitely on the prowl and the last thing they wanted was to meet a grateful husband, especially this husband. They thanked me, in return, dropped off the wall into the open country back of us, and disappeared.

And I, with the blood singing through my veins, knew that I would not be far behind them.

I looked across at Enrique, who was watching me steadily, and signaled to him that I was dropping down into the crowd again, but he shook his head and formed the words, "Not yet" with his lips. I pretended not to see and shifted my position sideways, as though looking for an opportunity to jump. And once, because I couldn't help myself, I looked back at Nita and said good-bye in my heart. Then watching the procession surreptitiously, I waited for a heavy concentration of marchers to pass by me. In a matter of seconds they were there, their torches and tall hats cutting me briefly from Enrique's line of vision.

And in that fleeting interval, I lay flat on my back, rolled off the wall, and dropped into the darkness on the other side.

# Chapter 18

I ran back of the wall, stumbling in the darkness, feeling drunk with elation. My release seemed decreed by Fate. Hadn't Enrique been forced to park in the most advantageous spot for me, outside the village, by the road that led to the main highway? With his arrogant habit of leaving his keys in his car, he had literally handed me my means of escape. A present from Enrique, I thought, and a bubble of near-hysterical laughter rose in my throat.

I had no passport and no driver's license, but if I could make it to Lugo, Edward would arrange everything. And, oh, what a joyful thing it was to be free, even for an instant!

Reaching the end of the wall I stopped, breathing hard. The car was less than half a block away, parked at the edge of a field, near the road; and the light, streaming through a cluster of pines at the entrance to the main village street, was filled with shadows, which gave excellent cover.

Now.

Crouching low and running between cars, motorbikes, and carts, I reached the car and crept into it on the darkest side. Alight with excitement and unease again, I felt for the keys on the floor. I had a sickening moment wondering whether I could drive. My fingers, wet with perspiration, fumbled badly with keys and ignition, losing precious time for me. Once I started the engine, I backed up and swung out into the road, easy enough at the wheel.

I switched on the distance lights, longing to press the accelerator to the floorboards; but I forced myself to increase my speed with nerve-racking care. The road was impossible, a dirt one, rutted from the rain and barely two lanes wide. It curved and wound in and out among the trees. I kept hitting these curves without warning, as there were no highway signs. Before I'd gone a kilometer, I felt the beginnings of a painful pull between my shoulder blades.

At the next curve, a right angle turn, I was compelled to slow down. My road now ran along the bank of the estuary and seemed to be the counterpart of the one that led into the Fuente estate on the opposite side of the *ria,* so I was sure, at least, that I was heading toward the main highway.

As I drove I listened unhappily to the sounds of the estuary, a frightening place by night. The tide was in and there was the heavy slap of water against the banks and the ominous song of water running in the grassy marshes.

Urgency was setting my blood on fire, but it was impossible to make time here. The road was too dangerous and narrow and there was the threat of a miscalculation. And below me on my right were the cold, dark waters of the estuary.

I crept along, watching the rearview mirror, eaten up with the longing to get to the main road. When I reached it at last, I was forced to stop and look for maps, losing more time I couldn't spare. But at least I knew that Lugo had to be southeast, away from La Coruña.

Finding maps in the glove compartment, I studied them by the light from the dashboard, holding their edges with stinging fingertips, afraid to turn on the overhead light.

Lugo was southeast all right, a long way southeast.

I saw that Enrique and I had followed a coastal road the night we'd come from La Coruña. I would have to retrace a discouraging distance before I could curve off toward Lugo, which was not on the main road between La Coruña and Madrid.

A large drop of rain splashed against the windshield and I jumped as though I'd been struck. I stuffed the maps back into the glove compartment, leaned out the window, and looked back down the lonely estuary road.

No lights. Not yet. I felt the perspiration on my face turning ice cold in the wind.

I shifted into gear, made a left turn onto the coastal highway, and picked up speed. This road was paved and considerably wider than the one I'd just left, but it was still only two lanes. Passing would be difficult but if I could get far enough ahead, this would be an advantage rather than a drawback. Enrique was an expert driver and a man who took chances, and I fervently longed for a heavy flow of traffic, both behind me and from the opposite direction, to keep him locked in position.

To my relief I saw several cars filling in in back of me, and I set a fast pace and thanked my lucky stars for Enrique's powerful car.

But the painful jubilance that I'd felt in the first moments of my escape were giving way to an anxious judgment of my situation.

Certainly for now I had the advantage, but one mistake I never made was to underestimate my "husband."

Still, Enrique couldn't start looking for me until the procession was over, and thinking I was in the crowd, he'd lose time searching. Once he realized I was gone, he'd have to find Alfredo and locate the Mercedes, which must be parked on the other side of the village, because it certainly hadn't been in sight on this side. If there were no road that led around the village, Enrique would lose more time waiting for the crowds to thin, so that he could get through.

Thinking of all this, my gnawing anxiety returned. And rain began to come down in long slanting lines, hampering visibility. I was disturbed to see, too, that when I reached the Madrid turnoff, the main body of the traffic seemed to be swinging in that direction.

The highway was relatively open now, and I knew I'd be no match for Enrique here. He must know this road by heart and driving in the rain came as naturally to him as breathing. I glanced up in the mirror and looked longingly back toward the road to Madrid.

Enrique, knowing my need for help in a

hurry, would, of course, guess that I was headed straight for Lugo and Edward. If I could have risked switching off toward Madrid, I would have had a better chance of getting away. But it was a full night's drive. More money would be needed, more gas. . .

For the first time since I'd gotten in the car, I glanced at the gas gauge, and then, stricken, stared at it, not believing. I had less than an eighth of a tank, and the needle was swaying dangerously toward empty.

This discovery gave me a jarring shock. I had gas for a good many kilometers yet, but I hadn't seen a single pump or station so far, and some of the wayside villages I'd passed through were already locked up tight, with just an occasional gleam of light through a closed shutter. Dark, dead-looking villages.

I felt a smothering panic rising in me; but there was nothing to do but keep going as fast as I could, and stop when I saw a station. And there I'd be in full view of anyone passing on the highway.

I kept watching the mirror as I drove. Four cars, some distance behind me. No way to tell how fast the ones in the rear were moving up, no way to know whether one of them was Enrique.

I drove on for what seemed a long time, through heavy rain and unlighted night, uncertain now whether I would ever reach Lugo and Edward. And as I drove a kind of slow despair spread through me. Because of my bad luck with the gas, the scales were tipping in Enrique's favor now. But I wouldn't give up.

Still, I had grown so discouraged and exhausted that seeing lights ahead, dimly, through a blurry windshield, meant nothing to me at first. When I realized that I was approaching a country hotel with a rusty looking gas pump out in front, tears of relief spilled out of my eyes and ran down my cheeks.

I dashed the tears away impatiently, and cheered and alert again I studied the cars in back of me in my mirror. The nearest one was a comfortable distance behind me.

The hotel, dully illuminated by three small lights over its entrance, was located at the end of a row of stone houses, all dark. I drove on past the hotel, looking anxiously about me; and when I saw a rocky patch of open ground a short distance beyond, I swerved from the highway at right angles, and went bumping off toward a grove of pines. This was just the kind of place I was looking for. I wanted to hide and watch the road for a while before I returned to the pumps and the lighted area.

I parked in under the wet whispering trees, turned off my headlights and engine, and counted myself lucky for the moment. Then I rolled down my window far enough to get a good view of the highway.

A small Fiat passed first, and an Opal soon after. Then nothing else for some time, while I sat shaking in the misty wind from the open window, never taking my eyes from the road. A truck, laboring under a huge load, came next; and then, at last, a long black Mercedes, traveling at top speed, a nightmare car, carrying two men. I'd gotten only a watery glimpse as the car passed under the hotel light, but I was sure of the car and the men.

Enrique and Alfredo, driving as though pursued by the Furies, hunting me down.

# Chapter 19

I rolled up the window but went on shivering, waiting there in the rainy dark, feeling as though I'd had a blow across the heart.

Perhaps, after all, there was no way to escape this man, this strange demon "husband," who drove like the wind and seemed determined to keep me close to him, no matter what the cost to anyone.

But wasn't this just exactly the way Enrique wanted me to think?

Well, I wouldn't do it; and I wouldn't give up so easily. I sank deeper into my coat, reminding myself that I was lucky to have worn something so warm, lucky that I'd found the gas pump after all. Seeing Alfredo and Enrique had been a shock, but I'd known they couldn't be far behind me. And when they reached Lugo they'd find a baffled Edward who couldn't tell them a thing, even if he'd been so inclined, which I was sure he wasn't.

There would be nothing for them to do but retrace, returning along this road. By then I would have bought my gas and would be hiding out again, waiting for them to pass. Not finding me in Lugo, they would have to consider three possibilities, it seemed to me: that I had taken the Madrid turnoff; that I had gone into La Coruña or in the opposite direction on the coastal route to some place like Santander; or that I had managed to hide in a small *pensión* somewhere. In any of these cases they'd need daylight and/or the Guardia Civil to find me.

Knowing Enrique, I was sure that he would wait for daylight and continue the search himself. He liked doing his own hunting, and he would want to avoid the humiliation of admitting to his Guardia Civil friends that he had a runaway wife.

By my rather haphazard reckoning, it would take Enrique and Alfredo perhaps thirty minutes each way to Lugo, and some minutes more locating Edward when they reached there. I was safe enough for the time being.

Still it was hard for me to start the engine and leave the sheltering darkness of the trees.

By the time I'd bounced back over the

rocky side yard to the hotel and drawn the car up in front of the pump, tears of nervous exhaustion had sprung back into my eyes. Dim as the overhead lights were, I felt horribly exposed, as though a spotlight had been turned on me. I unpinned the envelope inside my slip and once again counted my little sheaf of *peseta* notes, while I waited for the man inside the hotel lobby to come out and fill the tank.

I decided I would buy only half a tank of gasoline, which was more than enough to get me to Lugo, There was no way of knowing what the extra money might be needed for.

The seconds ticked by and still there was no sign of anyone from the hotel. When I couldn't stand it any longer, I honked the horn. More seconds passed and then a man came out of the door and crossed through the rain to the car.

"*Buenas noches, señor.*"

"*Buenas,*" he replied shortly, and when I asked for the gas, he sent me a curious hostile stare, and went around to the gas tank without another word.

I had long since learned that the Gallego reserved his warmth for his friends and had no time for strangers; and a woman traveling alone at night had about the same status here as a stray cat. But I could never quite believe these rebuffs, and I kept bruising myself against the hard, unyielding personalities of these people; and there had been the curiosity, which was disturbing. Anticipating this I had pulled my coat collar up as high around my face as possible, but I knew these unfriendly eyes had taken me in thoroughly.

To make matters worse, the delicious aroma of *caldo,* the strong Galician soup that I had become fond of, came through the open door of the hotel. Remembering that I'd barely touched my dinner, I realized how hungry I was. I didn't dare go into the hotel, and if I had dared, I couldn't afford to eat.

The man came back to my window and I thrust a bill at him. He stood in the rain in his shirt sleeves making change as deliberately as if the sun were beating down on him at high noon. We bade each other a brief and surly good night, and I got away as fast as I could, making a noisy departure and driving off down the highway in the direction I had come from, away from Lugo.

After I'd gone some distance I swung around, came back past the hotel at low speed and with dimmed lights, slipped back into my hiding place, into my cocoon of darkness. I felt reasonably safe here and in a sudden, non-caring reaction from strain, I almost slept.

But not quite.

When the Mercedes came back . . . after how long I had no way of knowing . . . now slowed down for more careful searching, cruising ominously through the misty night, fear seemed to melt the bones in my body. No matter that I had expected Enrique and prepared for him; that nightmare car gave me a fresh hard shock each time I saw it.

I watched as Enrique drew up by the gas pump and Alfredo got out of the car and went into the hotel. All just as I'd imagined it might be, and I had a horrifying feeling that if Enrique turned his head he would see me, see through the dark, hear the beating of my heart above the whisper of the pines.

Alfredo was gone scarcely a minute and then he was back again, bringing the hotel proprietor who stood talking to Enrique for some time. Then Alfredo got hastily back into the car, and the Mercedes moved off down the road toward La Coruña, gathering speed with a rush.

I let out a long hurting sigh, forced myself to remain there in the dark for a full five minutes. Then, at last, I reached out and turned the key in the ignition, and the car leaped forward.

The end of my journey was in sight.

As I drove toward Lugo I felt a sharp elation; but I was lightheaded from hunger, and I found it difficult to concentrate on my driving. There was almost no traffic now, however, and the rain had turned to mist, so I made good time, in spite of everything.

I felt as though I were flying instead of driving though the mist-streaked night, away from Enrique, whom I had evaded after all . . . to Edward.

It occurred to me to wonder that I put such faith in a stranger, that I accepted his offer of sanctuary without question. Was it just that he was so right and kind, or did he remind me of someone from that forgotten life of mine?

I found myself climbing a steep hill, and then without warning I was in Lugo.

It was a lovely place, rocky and uneven; and in its center was a beautiful cathedral. There was a Roman wall too, a magnificent one, that looked to be thirty or forty feet high. Even in my preoccupation I felt the impact of the town's ancient strength.

I slowed the car, listening to the wind singing in the chestnut trees around the square, enchanted with the stone houses, mellow and glowing in the light of the street lamps, their slate rooftops dotted with patches of moss, like fat green cushions. And I liked the town for its liveliness. People were walking in the streets and visiting together everywhere.

I drove cautiously around the square, finally spotting the one hotel, the Méndez Núñez. I parked the car, got out, and walked blindly through the lobby of the hotel, thinking only one thought: I had made it to Edward, at last, and this, somehow, was a homecoming.

When I reached the desk, the clerk wished me a brisk "Good evening" and cocked his head attentively, waiting for me to speak.

"I wish to see Señor Meredith, please."

"Señor Meredith is not here, señorita."

"Then I'll wait. Or perhaps he's in the dining room?"

"You do not understand. He is no longer in this hotel. He is in Madrid."

I reached out, caught hold of the edge of the counter, and hung on until the wave of dizziness passed. Edward's not being here was a possibility I'd never let myself consider for an instant, so that now I couldn't believe what I'd heard, couldn't believe what was happening to me.

The clerk said uneasily, "There is a letter. Perhaps it's for you. Perhaps you are this one . . ."

He reached in a box, pulled out a long white envelope, and laid it on the desk. On the front of the letter was the word, "Lisa."

"Yes," I said, and I had to bite my bottom lip to stop its trembling. "This is for me."

I put out my hand, trying not to snatch the letter; but it's hard to keep from snatching at a lifeline when you feel cold waters closing over you.

"Thank you, señor," I said in a whispery voice.

"It's nothing," he replied, sounding relieved. "My pleasure."

I stuffed the precious letter in my coat pocket, turned and fled back to the car. Once inside, I ripped the envelope open in a single movement, spilling its contents out into my lap. There were two thousand *peseta* notes and a sheet of paper with a few scrawled lines that read: "Lisa, I've been sent back to Madrid on business and am staying at the Hotel Valazquez. If you need me, contact me there. Edward."

I put my head down on the cold steering wheel and rested for a moment, my whole body limp with relief.

Not making contact with Edward had been the most shattering disappointment I could remember, but my upset world was now beginning to right itself again. It was a seven- or eight-hour drive to Madrid, but I had the money to get there now. I couldn't go much farther tonight, however. I must stop somewhere and eat, perhaps at an obscure *pensión* outside of town; and I would take a room there and hide out for the night.

But right now I wanted to get out of Lugo. The old feelings of anxiety and urgency had returned; and the street lights that had seemed comforting a short time ago were now too bright, too revealing.

I took out my map again, and studied it; reminding myself as I did so that Enrique was speeding away in the opposite direction. But he would have learned from the hotel clerk that Edward had gone on to Madrid, and I found this upsetting. I started the engine quickly, circled the square, and when I had located the road out of town that connected up with the through highway between La Coruña and Madrid, I was on my way.

I felt more peaceful when I was settled behind the wheel and moving again; and the driving was easy here because the road was deserted, but at the same time reasonably well lighted. My exhaustion, though acute, was almost welcome; it threw a pleasant dreamlike lassitude over me.

Perhaps that was why I was so slow in seeing it . . . the long black Mercedes that pulled from a cluster of oaks as I passed and fell soundlessly into line behind me.

# Chapter 20

If the earlier shocks I'd sustained in my nightmare flight were shattering, this one was annihilating, and when the Mercedes drove out around me and stopped some distance ahead, I recognized my bitter defeat. Incapable of connected thought now, I pulled over on the shoulder and cut my engine.

Enrique got out of the Mercedes, and Alfredo took his place in the driver's seat. Then Enrique walked back toward me through the mist, looking tall and sinister in the wet golden shine of the headlights.

My demon husband, from whom there was no escape, was taking me home for the last time.

As Enrique reached my car and jerked open the door it seemed to me that I heard the final curtain come crashing down on my life, and I put my head down on my knees and wept, crying with all the fierce abandon of a grieving child.

He got into the car, and I moved to the other side of the seat, as far away from him as possible. He neither spoke nor started the engine. He sat in silence while my sobbing filled the car with its ugly sound.

"Lisa, Lisa," he said wearily. When the sobbing went on, he reached out and laid his hand against my hair. I felt as though a hot brand had been applied to my head. I recoiled, my tears drying up in an instant.

I wanted no sympathy from my enemy.

The hand was removed with a jerk and he started the car, swung around, and headed back through Lugo. He looked almost as exhausted as I felt. Excellent. And I hoped Alfredo was in a state of collapse.

"How did you find me?"

"You're not all that hard to follow," he answered coldly. "The man at the hotel said you'd bought gas a little while before we came back from Lugo, but he didn't know which way you'd gone. We told him to keep a watch while we went up the La Coruña road and had a look. When we returned he said you'd been parked under some trees all along and had finally headed off for Lugo."

Enrique made it all sound so easy and inevitable. I hadn't had a chance from the beginning.

We settled into the long drive back and I

leaned my head against the seat and slept intermittently, haunting, disagreeable little naps. Once when I awakened, I saw that the sky was still black above the mist, but the stars were dying and a cold dawn was in the making.

The return trip seemed to go on forever. When it ended finally, Enrique brought me, stumbling with weariness to my bedroom door. There was a bright fire burning in the fireplace, my bed was turned down and Paca was waiting, fully dressed.

I'd never been happier to see anyone. I greeted her warmly. All this in rapid Spanish, and all in front of Enrique. He showed no surprise, and I noted this in passing, but I no longer cared. By attempting to run away I had made my position clear to everyone. There was no need to pretend about anything any longer.

After my enforced return to Enrique's house, I counted each threatening hour, with fear singing a terrible song all about me. The last dangerous, decisive days had begun. According to my anxious calculations, Enrique's California offer would expire in a bare two weeks. I thought I could feel the murderer growing restless in the wings, and, although Enrique made no moves, he watched me unceasingly. Was he hoping for one last bit of irrefutable evidence?

Edward was my only hope now. I could not escape without outside help, because the house guard had, of course, been re-alerted. For the first few days after my being brought back, I managed to get into town each afternoon, as usual, however. There, I waited for Edward with increasing desperation.

At my request, Paca always accompanied me into the village. I could not bear to be alone with Alfredo, and there was no question of Isidoro's substituting these days, I never spoke to Alfredo except to exchange cold greetings. I could not forget the evident intentness (and pleasure?) with which he had helped Enrique pursue me the night I tried to escape. Surely, I hadn't been worth Alfredo's best effort; at the last, I'd prove as ineffectual as the rabbits he hunted with such enthusiasm.

Once we arrived in the village, Paca and I would walk around and around the plaza, or we'd sit at the sidewalk cafe having tea.

We had nowhere else to go, because my favorite bench, across the street from the decaying house where I had seen Antonia that day, had become untenable. Any time I settled there, that same strange old lady would appear on her balcony, muffled in black shawls, to stand staring down at me, never taking her vicious, unblinking eyes from my face.

One afternoon, just as Nita joined us, Father Fernando rattled up to the cathedral in his old car. I hadn't seen him since the day we'd had our argument about the locked door, and I felt shy at meeting him again.

He got out of the car, and covered the awkward moment with a cordial invitation to come and make the official tour of his church.

"We kept hoping you would return, señora," he said.

I accepted in Nita's and Paca's behalf, as well as my own, delighted to put off the moment of our return home; and walking through the dusky candlelit aisles, I felt safe and peaceful for a little time. But even here the world intruded, and Father Fernando ended his recital in a troubled voice.

"The church is of great antiquity and beauty, as you see. But its own age and the damage it sustained during the Civil War have marked it deeply."

He reached out and pulled a crumbling piece of plaster from the wall, and a shadow, almost of physical pain crossed his face.

I turned away and thanked him hastily for our visit. Selfishly, I could not allow the intrusion of another's sadness. I hoarded my strength like a miser, knowing I had great need of it, if I were to survive.

My already impossible situation inside the Fuente family worsened daily.

Just as I had thought, my flight had amounted to a declaration that I considered myself a prisoner, and the fact that I had been forced to return verified this. Any pretense that I was in the Fuente household except under duress was ridiculous. The masks came off and feelings that had been held in check, boiled to the surface.

Carlos was the first to make his position clear. He waylaid me in the *galería* one evening, as I went between Nita's room and mine.

The exchange was necessarily brief, because it was just before the dinner hour. But he had seen me go down to Nita, evidently, and had kept his door open in order to catch me as I returned.

Stepping into the *galería,* he tried to block me off at the top of the stairs again, but I was too quick for him this time. And I was through with that silly uncle-niece routine.

"If you come near me, Carlos," I said in a voice that sounded as though it had come off an ice cap, "I'll rouse the household. What's more I'll tell them exactly what my reasons are."

"I don't know what you're talking about," he lied, his eyes narrowed with hate, "but there's something I have to say to you: I want those papers signed. Enrique may be able to put up with this nonsense, but not I. I want out of this hellhole and back to Madrid where I can live in a civilized way, and you're keeping me from getting there. I advise you to do as I say if you value that pretty little neck of yours. *Sign the papers.*"

Evidently, Enrique hadn't informed Carlos that there was an easier way of laying hands on the money. Certainly I had no wish to advertise this horrifying fact.

Frightened of Carlos in spite of my contempt, I said what I knew would sting the most. "So Enrique refuses to subsidize you while you live luxuriously and lazily in Madrid? What a pity!"

"I don't need subsidizing, damn you. I'm due a share of that money as a member of this family, and I'm going to get my part, one way or the other."

"Try the water torture," I said, but my brave reply belied my feelings, and Carlos knew this, because his next words were more threatening still.

"I'll think of a way . . ." he went on, smiling a little.

He was interrupted by a door opening across the *galería*. The grandmother stood in the doorway. She was dressed for dinner in rich black silk; she wore a single strand of pearls.

"Good evening, Lisa," she said in that tinkling voice that was so much a part of her fragile elegance.

"Good evening," I answered, with a shiver of relief at sight of her.

"And Carlos," she murmured.

She sent him a burning glance, then her lids lowered swiftly, her eyes now no more than gleaming angry slits. Without question she had heard at least part of what Carlos had said. The interruption had been deliberate.

"Good evening, Mother," Carlos replied, and a curdled flush came up in his cheeks. "Lisa and I were just passing the time of day."

The grandmother neither looked at him nor answered.

"Time to dress for dinner, I expect," he floundered on, trying for his usual brusque heartiness, pretending to consult his watch, as his whole face turned a dark unhealthy red. "Yes, indeed, must be off," he finished desperately, escaping into his room.

After Carlos' ignominious retreat, I stood looking at the grandmother, thinking how deftly she had broken up the ugly little scene between Carlos and me. More important, she had taken my part against him, sending him a silent, but I was certain, effective warning against harassing me further.

I wished to thank her, but I did not dare. Later I was glad I had not, because her next remark, an inquiry as to whether I had spent a pleasant afternoon, showed me that she was going to slide neatly over the incident, pretending nothing had happened.

"Yes, indeed," I answered, as polite as she, but deeply disappointed. For an instant I had thought that the grandmother and I were on the verge of sympathetic contact at last. Apparently not. Still, I waited expectantly.

But all she said was, "Splendid!" Then she turned back into her room and closed the door softly behind her.

By the time I had finished dressing, one of my wicked headaches had begun. I ignored it.

These headaches were becoming more

frequent and more intense as the days went by, and this frightened me. Deep in my brain I heard the warning. But my conscious mind refused to listen, because I didn't dare let down for an instant. Not with Enrique watching.

He even suggested that it was not necessary for me to put in an appearance at meals, but I wasn't falling into that trap. I knew that he wanted me to appear ill and languishing before the servants. Witnesses to back up his grim record. I refused my role as convalescent and often went down to dinner half blind with pain.

One evening after a particularly harrowing session, I found myself alone in the drawing room with Antonia. The grandmother had retired early and Enrique had gone off to his study to wait for a long-distance business call. Carlos, thank heavens, hadn't shown up at all.

"The Guardia Civil were here today," Antonia remarked casually. "It seems they're no nearer to solving Feli's murder than they were in the beginning."

"Yes, I saw them on the grounds."

I had been temporarily comforted, seeing them there, although I knew I would not be allowed any contact with them.

After Feli's death, both the servants and

the family had been interviewed by the Guardia Civil (most amicably, I was sure); but Enrique had begged off in my behalf, saying I was too ill to be disturbed. The matter of the red coat had had to be explained, of course. Enrique had questioned me, then relayed my answer to the police, where it was accepted without question.

They had obviously felt no need to press for an interview at a later date. Again, thanks to Enrique, I was sure. I felt certain that he had managed to establish that I was an unreliable witness because of my faulty memory. And having so recently arrived and knowing Feli only a short while, my lack of motive was apparent.

"The Guardia Civil say that Feli was killed, then dragged all the way from the avenue of trees to the *hórreo*, where she was lifted and carried up inside, on the ladder that's always there." Antonia's voice had all the detachment of someone at a tea party saying, "Please pass the cake."

I could feel the color draining out of my face, but I said nothing.

"For this reason, the police think that if Feli's murderer is a woman, she undoubtedly had an accomplice. But," Antonia added softly, "one can never be sure, can one? I've read of women, who, under great stress, exhibited manlike strength."

Antonia's intent was obvious. A sly and terrible accusation, designed to confuse and destroy.

"I've heard of such cases, but I give them little credence," I replied in a hating voice. "The accomplice theory seems much more likely. Incidentally, I believe you and Alfredo are often seen together."

A pale pink stain rose in Antonia's cheeks.

"I began coming here on visits when I was a child, so I've known Alfredo most of my life. He's a friend. If I occasionally go with him to a pigeon shoot, ride into the village with him, take a walk with him, whatever, I see nothing strange in that."

"I do. Taking a walk with him is one thing, but you were seen walking together at two o'clock in the morning, on the night of Feli's murder."

"By whom?"

"By me. I was on my balcony looking toward the *ria*. You and Alfredo came up the road in the moonlight."

It was a triumph, but a short one. Antonia's revenge was swift.

"Are you quite positive that you saw Alfredo and me that night? Enrique says amnesics are subject to fugues, to total blackouts, where they lose all sense of time and place."

"I have had no fugues," I replied coldly.

Antonia sent me a slanting look from under those beautiful lashes. "How can you be certain? The very essence of the fugue is the fact that you don't realize you're experiencing one. Where were you that night before you went onto the balcony? Were you on the balcony at all?"

Without another word, I got shakily to my feet and left the room. I would listen to no more of Antonia's grisly accusations.

But the damage had been done. When I reached my bedroom, Paca looked at me, and insisted that I take one of the green pills the doctor had left for me. As she helped me get undressed and into bed, I struggled to review again what Dr. Markam had explained to me about fugues. My brain felt on fire and I could recall only a line or two, but it was enough.

*. . . occurring after heavy stress, and fugues represent actual physical flight. The person wakes up in a strange place, having no memory of how he arrived there . . .*

I lay considering this eerie concept. I saw myself sneaking away from Paca and my room, fleeing outside my safeguards, not knowing that I did this, not knowing my destination, unable to recognize my enemies.

And perhaps the murderer, who had waited so patiently, would mark my going, and with an evil, satisfied smile, fall softly into step behind me.

# Chapter 21

Toward the end of that week, the rains began, falling in silver sheets, and by noon the days were as dark as twilight.

One lunchtime, while the rest of the family was seated near the fire, having the inevitable sherry, I stood at the drawing room windows listening to the sea breaking itself to pieces against the rocks along the shore, a fiercely desolate sound.

Enrique, who rarely sought me out now, came up beside me. "Our clothes have arrived from the States, and Juan will take your trunk to your room after lunch," he said. "I thought seeing your own things again might be pleasant . . ."

"Are you sure they're mine?" I asked deliberately.

He turned on his heel and went back to the others.

The arrival of the trunk proved to be one of the most diverting events that had happened in some time; and Nita who had not gone to school that afternoon because of a washout between the house and the village, arrived (duly accompanied by Anna) to help me unpack. Paca, for once shaken out of her placidity, stood by and kept up an excited running comment as we dragged the clothes out.

Nita, wearing a ski cap, a frilly white blouse that came to her ankles, and a pair of high-heeled red sandals, was very preoccupied with her work, and spent most of the afternoon upside down, delving and rummaging.

I did the sorting and the trying on; and each time I changed my dress, she looked up absent-mindedly and said, "Ravishing, my dear," and dived back into the trunk.

The clothes were more youthful and less expensive than the ones Enrique had bought me; but they had a flair. Trying them on, I felt a painful closeness to their owner, whom I had come to know better than my own forgotten self. Poor Lisa, I thought, poor betrayed Lisa.

I hung the dresses in the closet with care, and that evening I decided to wear one of them to dinner. The minute I had it on, I felt brave and determined, as though I were no longer alone. Lisa seemed to invade the room, an invisible, steadying presence.

The dress was an apricot chiffon shirtmaker with long sleeves and a flirty pleated skirt. I put on pale bisque lipstick, hung three golden chains around my neck, and went down to dinner.

Although I did so indirectly, I kept a close watch on Enrique as I came into the room. He was standing near the fire, and as I approached, a queer kind of stillness came over him. The blue eyes darkened, filling with shadows. There was no question that he remembered the dress and was shaken.

Yet he had stolen Lisa's identity and her name; and now, he was trying in the most horrifying way possible, to steal her birthright. Still, he must not be totally without conscience, and I guessed he spent a good many haunted nights trying to keep his private ghosts in order.

My headaches were so intense that I spent a great deal of time in my room, lying on my bed. Paca gave me one of the green pills almost daily. Afterward I would sleep, dreaming, with great sadness, of the man whose face I never saw.

I could not get into the village. Nita was having a long holiday now, and during that last terrible week, if Edward came for me, I never knew.

I went down to dinner every evening, but my headache went with me, and the pain of it had a way of lighting people up, making them unbearably clear.

Antonia, burning with her hate of me; the grandmother, so fragile and yet so powerful in directing and controlling the lives that came within her orbit; Enrique, withdrawn, watchful; Carlos, watchful, too, never coming near me now but always there, morose and dangerous-looking. I tried to protect myself from all of them by having Paca near me when I could, by spying, eavesdropping, listening always.

One evening, I heard Alfredo and Antonia talking together in the hall below me, as I went up the stairs. Alfredo's voice was ardent, beseeching, and Antonia's teasing and flirtatious, maddeningly elusive. Enrique had said that Alfredo was engaged; this fact seemed in no way to affect his feelings for Antonia. He sounded as though he were drowning in desire, willing to have Antonia on any terms, abjectly at her beck and call.

Perhaps he would do anything for her, if she promised enough. Would he murder for her? Had he? Agent of destruction or accomplice, it all came out the same. Listening to him now, it seemed to me that he would be willing to fill either role, for the price he asked.

The next morning, I was walking restlessly about the house while the maids turned everything upside down in the usual cleaning ritual. As I reached the end of the main hallway at the back of the house, I saw that the long windows on either side of the door were bright with sunlight. After days of rain, I found this flash of sun impossible to resist.

I stepped out on the terrace that faced toward the meadow and breathed cold sparkling air. My pleasure was marred, however, by seeing Alfredo coming down from the hills carrying a brace of dead rabbits.

I watched him against my will. He reached the back of the house, threw the rabbits down on the flagstones outside the kitchen door, and called imperiously to the cook. The rabbits lay with twisted legs and blood in their open mouths, and as Alfredo leaned over to wash his hands under the pump, I saw the water gush downward, and run over the flagstones, bright pink with blood.

I turned swiftly away, feeling a strange singing in my head, and then, instead of going back into the house as I meant to, I went down the terrace steps and off toward the hills.

I awakened, startled at the darkness around me, at the feel of wetness everywhere, and I told myself that it was night, that I must be sleeping. But my eyes were wide open, and when I moved my hand I felt rock under me, running with rivulets of water. Cautiously, I reached upward and not far above me was another layer of stone. I realized that I was lying flat on my back in a place like a rocky grave, and I wanted to scream and scream.

But I didn't dare.

Who had put me in this terrible dripping place, and was he still close by?

For a long time I lay breathing as softly as I could, feeling calmer as I realized that the air was fresh around me. Finally, reaching out on one side, I felt openness, and I saw that the darkness had a luminous quality. There was diffused light coming from somewhere, and I heard the sound of running water. There was a river nearby.

I saw that the greenish light was coming through a fissure in the wall opposite me, an opening just wide enough for a person turned sideways to pass through.

I must have gotten into this place through that fissure.

I seemed to be in a small stone room, lying on a shelf outcropping from the farthest wall. This shelf appeared to be about as high as a man's head and three or three and a half feet under the ceiling. Reaching down, I touched the rocky base that supported the shelf, and felt jagged, uneven rocks up its side that would make excellent footholds.

Unable to bear the silence and the dripping darkness any longer, I managed to raise myself on one elbow; and turning over, I dropped one leg over the shelf and found my first foothold. Then I climbed down the base of the shelf, backward, to the stone floor.

Still hearing no sound from the area outside, I crossed to the opening; and hiding well back in the darkness, looked out into a tremendous cave.

Glancing up I saw where the light came from. High above, sunlight fell from a hole in the ceiling, losing its strength in darkness. But I could see the faint, ghostly outline of limestone rocks, icicle-shaped stalactites, and ragged walls running with water.

This was the River Cave, the one Enrique had warned me about the day we quarreled on the hill.

Moving with care, I stepped silently into the cave; and still standing in the shadows against the wall, I looked and listened for the person who had brought me here. There was no one to be seen, no sounds except those of the dark murmuring river, the drip of water, the whine of cold winds among the stalactites.

How had I come to be in such a place? The last thing I remembered was running down the steps from the terrace of the house, alone.

Then I knew that no one had brought me here. Blind, lost in a fugue, I had come here on my own. But the eerie, bone-chilling part was imagining myself coming into this cave where I had never been before, climbing up to my gravelike place, and hiding there in the wet dark.

Worse yet, I remembered nothing of the person I had been during that stolen time, of that person's thoughts or actions. And how long had I been here. Hours? Minutes?

I could see moderately well now, and locating the stream that ran through the center of the cave, I followed along its bank until I saw, in the distance, the entrance that led to the outside world.

I began to run, stumbling, terrified by the echo of my own footsteps.

When I reached the opening, I burst out of the cave and sank down on a patch of grass that held the last warmth of the day. I sat there for a long time, forcing myself back into stillness, taking deep, long breaths.

It was late afternoon and I had been gone since morning. I would have been missed, and searchers would be out. I got slowly to my feet and tried to pull my clothes into some semblance of order. No one must know about the fugue, and I hoped that I might get past the searchers, and to my room before I was seen.

I found the path that I knew must lead upward to the meadow, but before I'd gone fifty yards along it, my hopes of getting to the house unnoticed were dashed. From a distant hill I saw Alfredo looking down on me, and before I'd gone another few yards I met Enrique face to face.

At sight of me he drew up, put one hand against the trunk of a tree and stood there, breathing heavily. His eyes swept over me, and then he glanced down quickly.

"Are you all right?" he asked.

"Yes."

His body had a pulled look, as though the skin had been tightened over his bones, tightened too much.

"And where did you find yourself," he

235

asked softly, "when you came to?"

I gave him a startled glance, knowing I must lie, realizing what explosive material he had come upon, if he guessed about the fugue.

Willing myself to speak normally, I said, "I didn't 'find' myself anywhere. I decided to explore the River Cave."

Enrique looked at me. "The big cave with the river running down its center?"

"Yes. The one you pointed out to me from the top that day."

"Not many people like going there alone. Wasn't it a little frightening?"

"A little, yes," I tried to speak casually, every word an effort.

Enrique did not say anything. Instead, he took out his handkerchief, dipped it in an indentation in a rock where water had collected and came over and washed my face. "You need to be a bit more presentable before we reach home, I think."

This precaution turned out to be unnecessary. The grandmother had not been told I was missing and was still in her room, and Nita was at school. Paca, Nita's señorita, the maids, the two gardeners, and even the cook were out combing the area, and Alfredo was just now in the process of rounding them up.

As we went up the stairs, I swayed with weariness, but remembering the doubt I'd heard in Enrique's voice when I mentioned exploring, I said as briskly as I could, "I went some distance back into the cave. Very interesting."

"And what did you discover that was so interesting?" Enrique asked carefully, as he supported and guided me across the *galería.*

"Well the strange lighting from the hole in the roof. Eerie, of course, but I expected that. Then there's that odd little room off the main cave that one enters through a fissure in the wall."

Enrique's fingers tightened on my arm. He stopped and pulled me around to face him, his brows drawn together in a puzzled frown.

"What odd little room? Alfredo and my cousin and I spent half of our boyhoods exploring the River Cave. We never, at any time, saw such a room."

"It's small and dark, and there is a shelf of stone, just below the ceiling."

Enrique continued to gaze at me. Gradually, the questioning look faded from his face, his eyes darkened.

"There *is* such a room," I insisted desperately.

"How sad you are," he said. Then, almost

as though he were unaware that he did so, he reached out and laid the palm of one cool hand against my hot cheek.

Perhaps it was a measure of my misery and confusion, but, strangely, I longed to reach up and press that strong, cool hand still harder to my face. It was with an effort that I turned away.

# Chapter 22

By eleven the next morning, Nita and I were taking a walk in the rain-streaked day. We wore *zuecos,* black slickers, and brimmed fisherman's hats. Even so, our constitutional was necessarily short because the *zuecos* made walking difficult, and we ended up resting on a waterlogged bench in the summerhouse.

Nita soon found this boring, and began circling the summerhouse on some mysterious errand of her own. I leaned my head back against the wall, exhausted by a wakeful night and distressed by fearful speculations about yesterday's lost hours.

Knowing such preoccupations to be dangerous ones, I concentrated on the rain clouds boiling across the sky, and listened to the exciting, crashing music of a high green sea. I considered how, under happier circumstances, I could have loved this wild land.

But it had been too late for this before I

ever arrived, and each day grew worse. This realization brought me full circle, back to my lashing fears, back to Enrique. I was sure he hadn't been deceived about yesterday's fugue. Would this regression of mine give him the final, dramatic proof he needed for the "Lisa" folder?

Nita, glistening like a baby seal, came back into the summerhouse and lifted her rosy face to mine. "I heard you were lost yesterday, in the cave."

I answered as lightly as I could. "Who said so?"

"All the maids are talking about it. I heard them."

Enrique had lost no time in getting the latest bulletin out on me, then, and the household was teeming with the news. The servants must think me completely mad by now.

"I find it very cold here, Nita," I said, struggling to keep my voice from trembling. "Would you mind if we went in now?"

"Anything you say, my dear," Nita answered contentedly.

But if I thought to find any peace anywhere that day, I was mistaken. Nita and I, returning through the back way in order to dump our rain things on the servants' porch, had barely made it upstairs, when

Enrique stepped out into the hall, asked me politely and formally if he might speak to me, and returned to his study. Nita, who was scheduled to go calling with her grandmother after lunch, was taken off by her señorita for a proper scrub down. It was the señorita's half-day off, and she looked as though she didn't want to miss a second of it.

I stood for a moment collecting my courage; I refused to go cowering into Enrique's study, but I had never been more frightened in my life. As I stepped through the study door and got a glimpse of myself in a gold-framed mirror above the fireplace, I was pleased with the reflection that came back to me. My head was high and my cheeks flamed.

Enrique was standing behind his desk, frowning down at some papers. When I came in, he glanced up and then looked at me for a long time.

I looked back at him. He wore one of his American business suits, a conservative gray one, not very different from his Spanish clothes. I noticed with interest that the fit of the suit was less than perfect. He was thinner than in the San Francisco days. His skin, always pale, was paler still, and his heavy brows were like black brush strokes. Except for the blue eyes, everything about him was as stark and unrelieved as a charcoal drawing.

"I have a present for you, Lisa," he said.

"What is it?"

He reached into the pile of papers, picked up something and tossed it toward the edge of the desk.

"Your freedom."

I drew nearer, saw my passport, and reached out for it. "I — I don't understand."

"You'll never get well here. I realized that after your fugue yesterday . . ."

I clutched the passport in stiff fingers, listening with deep attention.

"I thought I could bring you home and make you whole again, but now I know that such a plan was hopeless from the beginning. Go back to San Francisco, Lisa. Being there and being with Dr. Markam again may be the answer."

I stood rigid, holding my alarm behind a blank face. I knew that I was being led into a trap, but what kind of trap I couldn't guess; I never ceased to be amazed at Enrique's ingenuity.

"And you want me to sign the papers before I go?"

"No. Keep the property in your name, temporarily. The oil income will see you through until you're settled. Call it alimony, a property settlement, whatever."

"Do you want a divorce, then?"

"What else is there?"

Still feeling my way in the dark, I asked, "And will your family agree to such an arrangement?"

"Yes. When I tell them what the plan is. When you marry again, you must sign the property back." And then he added with a strange little smile, "That won't be long, I imagine."

I stood looking down at my passport, but what I saw were my prison gates swinging open. Why? It was all too easy. And I knew that Enrique's family would never agree to this settlement of the property within days of the long anticipated sale.

I lifted my eyes again, feeling safer watching him. "And when did you want me to leave?"

"Today. This afternoon. Dr. Martinez, from the village, will take you to La Coruña to catch the plane to Madrid." He reached into the pile of papers and came up with a long envelope. "Money for tickets. And extra money for the journey."

With every word he uttered the situation grew stranger, and there was no way to know what lay beyond this strangeness. "You're not taking me to La Coruña, then?"

He snapped the fastener on his briefcase closed. "No. I have important business in Santander, and I must leave immediately."

I'd heard nothing of a business trip to Santander until this moment. I stared down at the briefcase with a rush of horror, realizing that it was just the right size to carry a folder full of papers. A folder labeled "Lisa?"

Yes, I expected that Enrique did have important business, business that would solve all his problems and ruin my life. I gave no sign of the shattering turmoil going on inside me, except to clutch my passport tighter. There was nothing to do but ride the crest of this thing until I could get my direction.

Enrique picked up the briefcase and came and stood in front of me.

"I ask only one thing of you, Lisa."

"What is it?"

"That you not leave with anyone but Dr. Martinez."

Not leave with anyone but a doctor? Did Dr. Martinez go often into La Coruña? Knowing how overworked and tied to the village he was, I guessed he almost never did so. I thought I was beginning to see the outlines of the trap; the implications took my breath away.

"Where will Paca be?" I asked carefully.

"She'll go back to the village. I told her there would be no further need of her services after today."

I wanted to turn away from him, but I made myself stand still, lowering my lids so that he couldn't see the terror in my eyes.

"All right. I'll do as you say." This promise wasn't meant to be kept. All I wanted was to get away from him.

"I'm sorry, Lisa. About everything." Then, without warning he leaned down and kissed my cheek. *"Vaya con Dios."*

I was alone, then, feeling, to my astonishment, a sense of loss. This feeling passed into anger when I heard Enrique run up the stairs, across the *galería.* A door opened and closed softly. I knew what part of the *galería* this sound came from. He had gone to Antonia's room.

I waited, not moving, listening. It was some time before Enrique returned to the lower floor. He went to the closet for his raincoat and then the front door opened and closed, and he was gone.

I sat down in the big leather chair nearest me, trying to bring my flying thoughts into some kind of order. In the end it came to this: There was nothing left to me but the choice between two dark paths.

I could go away with Dr. Martinez to La

Coruña, to whatever awaited me there. I was sure I would not get farther, not even as far as Madrid. Enrique's plan was coming clearer now, and it did not include my ever leaving La Coruña, I was certain. When I arrived there, *under the care of my doctor,* I would find my "husband" waiting. With his "Lisa" folder, of course, and with other doctors, already briefed and assembled. Had the money and the passport been given to me, to entice me on my terrible journey, to keep me tractable en route? I thought so.

If this choice did not suit, I had one other, I told myself bitterly.

Paca, my only safeguard would be gone; but I could refuse to accompany Dr. Martinez, and stay on in Enrique's house. I would not dare leave it, however. After what had happened to Feli, my old plan of making a night run into the town was unthinkable. Here, at least, Nita's presence offered some fragile protection. It was not enough, considering that a murderer was close at hand. I could almost hear him now, the careful footfalls on the dark stair. Or would he come in stockinged feet, so that his movements would leave no echoes in the lonely *galería?*

I was not long in deciding what to do. Dr. Martinez, even if he were strongly under the

Fuente influence, was not a part of this secret house. And whatever his purpose, he would be taking me into the outside world, away from this place of shadows. Yes, I would leave today.

Decision gave me courage, and I went to my room to pack. Paca was there, reading a new paperback, her overnight case open, and her second uniform already laid away in it. When she saw me, she got to her feet, twisting the book between her fingers, her face troubled.

"Señor Fuente has told me that you are going from us today, señora, that I am no longer needed."

"Yes, Paca. I will be leaving this afternoon. I understand Dr. Martinez will be coming for me later."

"After the time of the *merienda*, señora."

"Well, I must pack now, I think. I want to spend some time with Nita when she returns from her visiting."

"I will pack for you. Please, just to show me what's to be taken."

My unruffable Paca still wore her troubled face. I had never seen her disturbed before.

I went to the closet and began selecting the clothes I wanted, tossing them out onto the bed. I was taking only what had belonged to Lisa Stephens. The clothes Enrique had given me were left neatly hanging in their places.

"You go so suddenly, señora," Paca continued. "Many in the village have remarked upon this fact."

My fingers closed convulsively on a hanger. How was it that half the countryside seemed to be aware of my departure when I had barely heard of it?

"And how did the villagers have word of my going, Paca?" I asked as easily as I could.

"The señor told me last night that you would be leaving. I sent news to my family of this. Also, that I would be returning to our house tomorrow. You do not mind, señora?"

"Not in the least," I replied, wonderfully relieved that the matter stood so simply.

I had thought that for some frightening reason, Enrique might have advised the village of my going.

"Did the señor say anything more?" I inquired casually.

"Only that he considers you well enough to travel now." Paca looked at me doubtfully. "He thinks a little holiday would be beneficial to you. Is this so, señora? That you feel well enough for a holiday?"

Thinking of the holiday Enrique had in

mind for me, I found I could not speak. I tried to smile at Paca, as I turned again toward the closet.

When I came back to the bed with the last of Lisa's dresses, I said, "That's the lot, Paca."

"But, señora, you have left the most beautiful, the finest ones . . ."

"Please pack only the things I've laid out."

I could see why Paca was confused. Lisa's dresses, once assembled and folded, looked meager and unimpressive.

With one exception. The apricot chiffon. I packed it with care, feeling a grimness about my mouth. It was Lisa's wedding dress, I knew.

"Is that all you're taking?" a cool voice behind me asked.

"Yes," I answered shortly, turning to see Antonia standing in the open doorway. She wore a tweed traveling suit with a sable collar. She looked elegant and beautiful, and pleased.

"Then this is good-bye, I expect," she said.

"I expect it is," I answered, not giving an inch.

"For now, at least," she added, pulling on a silky, leather driving glove.

Where was Antonia going? Was she meeting Enrique in La Coruña . . . afterward . . . ?

Stunned by the possibility of such timed, calculated betrayal, I turned back to the bed, so that Antonia couldn't see my face. I felt like a ghost I'd read about in childhood, a ghost who had a burning coal for a heart.

"Good-bye, Antonia," I said, putting the last of my things into a suitcase. "And now, if you'll excuse me, I have to dress."

"Good-bye, Lisa," she answered, and I could hear the smiling triumph in her voice as she closed the door behind her.

I snapped the last bag closed and hurried into the bath, where I put on a white blouse and a navy traveling suit. Nita and the grandmother would have returned by now and there was no time left for anything but thinking of Nita.

What would I say to her, I wondered unhappily? How could I bear to tell her good-bye?

Explaining to Paca where I was going, I went out the door and crossed the *galería,* worrying all the way downstairs. I wouldn't, of course, tell Nita that I was leaving for good. That would only make the parting harder.

When I reached Nita's room I found her gone. I knew she had returned from the village because Anna was missing. Nita, who never went anywhere in the house without her boon companion, had dropped in to pick up her friend; I could only think that she had then gone to the kitchen for a snack, or perhaps the grandmother had sent her on an errand.

I was ridiculously disappointed. The time I had left to be with her was all too short, as it was. And I was surprised that she had returned home without coming to my room, as was usual when she had been away most of the day.

I looked about me, not certain what I was looking for, dreading to see. I found it soon enough, a note, written in smeary block letters, running up hill. It said:

DEAR TIA LISA, WE'RE TAKING A WALK IN THE RIVER CAVE, AND ANNA, TOO. YOU'D BETTER COME.

Nita

The note bristled with wrongness. I held it as though it might burst into flame, in my hands. Who was "we?"

# Chapter 23

I rushed out of the room, down the hall and up the stairs, calling "Paca! Paca!"

I found Paca hurrying across the *galería* toward me, her face filled with alarm. "Señora?"

"Have you seen Nita since she returned?"

The alarm subsided. "No, señora. Nita has not returned from her outing. As you know, she and Doña Carmen sometimes visit friends until late afternoon, and it is early yet."

"But Nita was here," I almost shouted. "Anna is missing."

"The doll, señora?" Paca looked at me oddly. "The doll could be anywhere — fallen behind a chair or . . ."

"No. No. The doll is always with Nita. And besides there's this note that Nita left me." I knew my voice was rising too urgently. Both Carlos and Antonia came out of their rooms, and stared at me.

Antonia had taken off her coat and gloves, but her luggage was waiting by the door. I had thought her long gone, since she had appeared on her way when I last saw her. She gave no explanation of the delay, but said evenly, "Could you please tell us what this incredible fuss is about?"

"Nita's gone off to the River Cave with someone, and under duress. You can tell by this note, which is a frightening one. We must search for her immediately, call out the household."

"No, señora," Paca tried to assure me. "There is no need. I have just come from the kitchen. The maids and the cook made no mention of seeing Nita, and as you know, she either comes to your room or goes to see the cook, when her Señorita is away."

"Let me see the note, please," Carlos said coldly.

I passed the note to him and he read it and handed it silently to Antonia. She also read it and then gave me a speculative glance. "This doesn't sound like Nita."

"Of course, it doesn't," I answered, almost in tears. "Someone told her what to write. That's why we must look for her. Now. This minute."

Antonia and Carlos exchanged guarded looks and then Antonia said, as though speaking to a child, "There is no need for all this disturbance. Nita is in the village with Doña Carmen. Neither of them has returned."

"Nita has been here. I know she has."

Carlos turned to Paca. "Paca, would you take Señora Fuente to her room and see that she rests before Dr. Martinez comes for her? Her unfortunate experience in the cave yesterday seems to be preying on her mind."

Before Paca could reach me, I ran to the grandmother's door and banged loudly on it; then I waited, wild with impatience, certain that she and Nita had returned. There was no answer.

"Come, señora."

I went with Paca then. Tears of frustration streamed down my face, but I knew I was only wasting time resisting. And I knew what they all thought . . . that I had written the note myself.

I lay still pretending to sleep, making my secret plans, waiting to be sure that Paca, settled down for her siesta, was sleeping. No one would believe me, no one would help me, and no one would let me go if my plans were known.

I was certain that Nita was in the River Cave. And if she were there she was counting on me, marking every passing second with a frightened heartbeat.

I knew something else, too. No matter what the danger to me, I couldn't leave her there, waiting on and on. Nita was not to be among the betrayed.

I'd see to that. And measuring my own terror against my love for Nita, I knew I could do what I had to do.

Paca's breathing had become rhythmic. Not yet, I thought, wait a minute longer, and I counted the seconds slowly and deliberately. Then I was up and out, carrying a pair of low-heeled shoes, running through the house in my stockinged feet.

So much time had been lost already, I told myself, as I paused on the terrace, slipped into my oxfords, and jerked and tore at the laces with trembling fingers. Ready at last, I went swiftly down the terrace steps and as rapidly as I could across the soggy, swollen ground. Thank God, the rain had stopped and the sun come out. That helped, but the going was difficult, and it was so much farther than I'd remembered.

And in spite of all my brave resolutions, fear slowed me down, fear for Nita, fear for myself, in that dark and dripping place.

I was almost there now, and long before I reached the cave entrance I began calling

Nita's name. There was no answer, no sign of her, no sound but that of the wind moving in the heather.

Then slowly it began to happen, an awareness of a too deep stillness all about me. I turned my head stiffly and studied the area where I was, looking out of the corners of my eyes.

It was some time before I found what I was looking for, and I moved nearer to make sure. Anna was lying just inside the cave entrance, half in shadow. Her doll's head was split wide open. One broken piece of face, with its single staring eye, was turned toward me; the other half of the head had rolled away into darkness.

I waited for a wave of dizziness to pass; then I moved noiselessly forward and stood staring down at Anna. Her cloth body had been hacked to pieces, leaving the cotton stuffing spilling out of her; but her severed legs were carefully lined up with the ravaged torso.

I took a deep aching breath and called as steadily and loudly as I could, "Nita!"

This time she answered, from somewhere back inside the cave, in a whispery, tear-drenched voice. "I'm here, *Tia*."

I ran through the cave entrance and straight toward the point where I thought her voice had come from, through the dripping, luminous darkness, eerily lit by light streaming from the hole in the cave's roof.

Then I saw her, huddled on a boulder well inside the cave, her sweater dark with wetness, her eyes shiny with tears.

I ran on, over the wet rocky floor of the cave; and she half fell from her rock and ran toward me, her arms outstretched. We met, and she caught me around the waist and wouldn't let go.

I leaned down, and knowing without conscious thought that I must whisper, I asked, "What happened to Anna?" But even the whispers set up little murmuring echoes and the cave was full of them.

Nita pushed her face against me, and her whispered, "She got hurt," was almost inaudible. But her terror, rising up around us like a mist, told me all the things she dared not say, told me the thing I had known in my heart, but could not let my mind recognize, lest I falter . . . that the murderer I had fled so long, and thought myself almost free of, was here, standing somewhere between us and the cave entrance, cutting off my escape, waiting in the dark.

Nita was only a decoy, I knew, the one lure that he had known I could neither refuse nor deny. And Anna, cut to pieces in the cave entrance was horrifyingly symbolic, making it clear the kind of person I dealt with.

My own fear was suspended now, or perhaps simply lost in my deeper fear for a helpless child, a child I loved very much. All my thoughts, all my energy, drove me toward one objective: to see Nita out of this tainted darkness and running free again. This, I knew, was what the murderer had counted on.

Praying that I reasoned correctly, that my stalker would find Nita a hindrance and distraction in his plans for me . . . that, since Feli's murder, he would be wary of having us both disappear . . . I leaned down and putting my mouth close to Nita's ear, said, "Turn toward the entrance and when I tell you to, begin to run, and don't stop, and don't look back."

Nita, in spite of all her shocks, was not without her own bright brand of courage; still clinging to me, she whispered back, "I can't leave you, *Tia*."

"But you must go for help."

I said this for Nita, knowing she must have a reason to go, knowing she must be set free of guilt. But for me there was no help.

It was a long way home for an exhausted child, and not much time is needed for a murder.

When my rescuers came, they would find the cave as they had always known it, a huge stone chamber filled with murmurings and capricious winds, its walls wet, its icy river running through darkness. I would be well asleep forever, and the echoes of my screams would have died away without a whisper.

With shaking fingers, I loosened Nita's arms from around me. "Be brave. Run fast. Now."

Nita ran, straight toward the cave opening.

And it was only after she had gone that I remembered she must know the identity of the murderer, and a moan of regret escaped me. But Nita's flight went unhindered. When she reached the cave entrance, someone called after her, "If you bring help, Nita, or if you ever tell anyone what happened today, I'll cut you up like Anna. Always remember Anna."

At the sound of the voice Nita faltered. Then she ran on, out into a day beginning to drift with rain again. As she ran, the echoes called after her, "Remember Anna . . . Remember Anna."

# Chapter 24

I had gone quiet, listening to the voice, hoping to identify it. But the echoes defeated me.

No matter. I would know my murderer soon enough, and now the terror, held in abeyance while Nita was with me, struck like a blow in the face.

I could hardly breathe. I turned toward the place where the voice seemed to be and found a pair of glittering eyes watching me. Then, there was movement, and a piece of darkness, breaking off from deeper darkness. At last, he stood before me, in the wet, green light, tall and still in his conical hat, his processional robes floating about him in the cave winds that came and went.

Father Fernando.

He was across the stream from me, a distance away. I could not turn or move or run. His brilliant gaze held me as though I were a newly impaled moth, motionless with shock upon my pin.

"Father . . ." I began, but the single word died among the echoes.

I thought of Anna's mutilated body, and I listened to the wind honing the deep recesses of the cave, and I felt a bat, disturbed in his dusky dreams, dart past my face.

"I regret what has to be done," Father Fernando said, speaking at last. "But my cathedral must be saved. You planned to go away, stealing what had belonged for generations to the Fuentes, destroying all of our hopes, taking the money Enrique had promised for the restoration of my beautiful church . . ."

Memory cut though my mind like a heated knife, and I thought of the day Father Fernando had shown me through the cathedral, of the way he had peeled plaster from a damaged wall, as though he were peeling away his own skin, of the pain in his face . . .

My voice was low, weighted with horror, but to me it sounded like a shout. "I'll sign anything, Father. I want nothing that isn't mine. I'll sign and go away. I'll never return."

I heard rasping, terrible laughter.

"It is of no importance to me what you sign. By Spanish law, since there are no children, everything you have goes to Enrique at your death. I care nothing for this family talk of signing papers. The simple solution, from the beginning, has been to kill you."

I recognized the easy, unhurried voice of a madman, reasoning without reason. "But it's all taken time. I'm not a good shot, and that day you moved just as I fired. Then there was the necessity of locking you in the church, to keep you from making a disastrous departure. To add to all this, there was the matter of Feli, a disturbing mistake. There will be no mistakes this time."

"Nita will tell," I said desperately.

"Nita will never tell because I will frighten her into silence. Your death will look like an accident. I shall drown you in the river, say that I found you there after I saw you walking in the hills, after I saw you fall through the hole in the roof. Don't you think I will be believed?" he finished tauntingly.

Yes, I thought he'd be believed, and I saw no way of escape. But the blood, frozen for so long in my veins, began to warm and flow again. My reviving body refused to go down into that cold, dark river without a struggle.

I began backing away, trying to get outside the dimly-lighted area of the cave, into the fringe of darkness behind me. Although the river was only a few inches deep, Father

Fernando must ford it before he got to me.

When he saw me move, he lifted his robes and started to run, coming at me in long, leaping strides, like a giant black spider. I turned my back on him and fled into the comforting darkness, stumbling along by the cave wall, trailing my hand along the wall as I ran, praying that Father Fernando hadn't brought a torch. Evidently he had not. He must have counted on dispatching me easily in the central part of the cave. Or perhaps, in his mad way, he had been preoccupied, as indicated by his ceremonial robes, with the sacrificial aspects of doing away with me.

One small score for me because his long wet robes must be hampering him.

He was stumbling behind me, searching, and there was no way among the echoes to know whether he was gaining in the dark. My body flowed with rivulets of chilled perspiration, the winds cut through my clothes, and icy droplets fell from the roof onto my face and hair. None of this mattered. I felt aloof and strange in my fear, as though I were another person, sitting high and safe on a rock, watching this poor creature struggling along below, fleeing without hope.

Not quite without hope, and this was enough to keep me going. Somewhere along this wall was a fissure, and through this fissure and beyond it was that small room, totally dark, with its shelf near the ceiling, to hide upon.

Enrique had said there was no such room, but I had been there. He had to be mistaken. And if Enrique hadn't known about the room, surely Father Fernando was not likely to.

Only I, with my conscious mind asleep and my fear-driven subconscious in charge, had been able to find this hidden room. How disturbed and haunted I had been when I had awakened yesterday from my fugue and found myself in such a place. And now I sought it as a sanctuary.

I was sure from the sounds behind me that Father Fernando was closer now; and I was beginning to slow down, leaning forward a little as I ran, like a person who discovers, to his surprise, that he is bleeding internally, but still stumbles on.

My other self, sitting high and safe, advised me that the chase was almost over, that the effort was too much, that I'd die in the end anyway.

That was when my hand touched emptiness, and I felt wildly across the wall for the boundaries of the fissure. I slipped through the wall and falling to the floor placed my head on my drawn-up knees and tried to force my labored breathing into silence.

Not a minute later Father Fernando went by, evidently wide of the wall. I was sure now that he didn't know about my room, but he knew the general layout of the cave, and he was going at a steady persistent pace. I was certain that he would circle and search and never give up until he found me.

As I climbed up on my shelf and lay down, I felt hot tears on my face. "Oh, Enrique . . ." I whispered, not knowing why I said this.

The search went on and I lay listening, feeling my heart leap with fresh terror at each new sound. I could place my pursuer fairly accurately because every dislodged rock, every scrape of shoe against stone sent out its own small echo. He was circling the cave again on his way back, moving more carefully now.

One more circle, and then I heard him plunging wildly through the river to the center of the cave. Here he let out a furious, hysterical shout. "I'll find you finally. Oh, yes, I'll find you . . . and when I do . . ."

"And when I do . . ." the echoes called, and I lay as still as the stone beneath me, listening. Already in my grave, I thought.

Father Fernando circled the cave again

and again, and the search grew quieter each time. There were long periods of silence when I knew he stood listening in the dark. Either that or he had made the circle so many times that he had become expert at moving soundlessly.

The silence was more terrifying than the shouting and the echoes, but I was becoming accustomed to having fear for a bedfellow. And in my exhaustion, once strangely, I almost slept. When I realized what I had done, my eyes flew open wide and I never closed them again. I lay on one side with my arm hanging limply down from the shelf, scarcely breathing.

Finally, after one of the longest silences of all, Father Fernando reached up and caught me by the wrist.

# Chapter 25

I screamed, a single shattering scream and the echoes screamed with me.

Above the echoes came men's shouts, the sound of running feet, and the glow of strong torches lighting the darkness outside my room, lighting the fissure opening. Through this opening I saw Father Fernando scuttling away.

Unable to believe the lights and the shouting, terrified that the clamor would melt back into silence, I rolled from my shelf, made my way painfully down its base, and stumbled to the opening.

But the sounds were there, growing louder, and above them all Enrique calling, "Lisa! Lisa!" and I picked this calling up out of the running and confusion.

Enrique. Not with Antonia, but here.

I turned sideways and half fell through the fissure, just as Alfredo, Pepe, and Enrique came to a ragged halt a few feet away.

I must have been an awesome sight, but I stood up as best I could and looked squarely back at them. Enrique's shadowed eyes took in every inch of me, and still he couldn't seem to look away, but all he said was, "My God, what a set of lungs."

Then I was forgotten and Father Fernando remembered again, as rocks fell somewhere in the distance. The torches swung in that direction and picked out Father Fernando climbing up the end wall of the cave, clawing his way up the farthest limestone face, making for the hole in the ceiling. Some of the rocks in the cave were smooth, rounded by the ceaseless drip of water. But the ones Father Fernando was crossing were talus rocks, ragged and sharp with falling, and he must have climbed with bleeding hands. His long robes ripped and shredded as he went and the wild cave winds sent them flying out behind him.

"Father," Alfredo shouted, "you'll never make it." But the words died in the fading echoes, and the black figure never paused. We stood transfixed, unable to restrain or help this mad old man, watching his painful progress up the razor-sharp cliff.

At last he reached a ledge near the roof and fumbled and slid, trying to climb onto it. Rivulets of water had made the ledge slippery, and it was some time before he managed to hoist himself up. Once there he huddled down, resting, watching. He had long since lost the conical hat, but he was grotesque enough, staring down at us from his distant perch.

"Father . . ." Alfredo shouted again, and as though the word had startled him into action once more, Father Fernando leaped to his feet and half-turned toward the cliff.

This turn was never completed. Caught in his shredded robes, he slipped on the wet ledge and plunged headlong over its edge, his arms outstretched before him. And before our unbelieving eyes, he fell slowly, silently, like some great doomed bird.

He hit face down in the icy river, and the water around him ran red and his black robes bubbled up around him.

I heard the sound of weeping and didn't know it was my own until Enrique grabbed me by the shoulders, turned me away, and led me out of the cave.

"Wait here. I must help Alfredo and Pepe with Father Fernando. I won't be long."

I stood in the entrance, watching him go back into the cave, feeling bereft as the space between us grew wider. Enrique was still wearing his business suit, and over this his American raincoat.

I put my hands to my temples and pressed hard, struck suddenly by a new kind of headache, one infused with a puzzling radiance. The radiance spread as I stared after Enrique, and although I was wide awake I seemed to be inside the dream I had dreamed so often in these last months, the dream of the man in the rain.

My breath felt light and quick. I watched Enrique with fascinated attention as he walked away from me. The same easy stride, the same tan trenchcoat, the black hair sparkling with rain in the streetlight . . . *no, the torchlight. . . .*

The radiance burst in my head like an exploding star. I called, "Enrique! Wait. Wait."

And I began to run.

He turned just as I reached him and we met with a hard satisfying impact. His arms went around me automatically. I clung to him, unable to speak, dazzled with disbelief, with the burning clarity of remembering.

I continued to cling, still silent until he pushed me a little away from him and asked cautiously, "What is it?"

Then the words began and I couldn't stop them.

"Oh, Enrique, do you remember that gray

apartment house on Nob Hill in San Francisco where I lived, and the night we quarreled about something and you were so angry, and how I ran down the steps to the street and called after you . . . ?"

It was his turn to be silent. "I remember," he said, at last, and his voice sounded as though he too held his breath as he waited, as he listened.

"And my apricot chiffon wedding dress? Do you remember? And how we were laughing together just before the accident?"

Suddenly his arms tightened about me in a fierce, possessive embrace.

"Lisa."

But I hardly heard, because the word was drowned out by the hard, excited pounding of our hearts.

Looking back later, it seemed to me that the walk home was one of the strangest and loveliest times I'd ever known.

The rain had stopped again, and dizzy with exhaustion and excitement, I felt as though Enrique and I walked a foot or two above the now starlit path. Even so, I seemed to stumble on air. Then Enrique would make me stop and rest; but he always stood apart from me. I understood why he did not touch me again. Our peace was too

271

new, the memory of pain too fresh.

Then we would start out again, and the words would pour from us once more, interrupting, explaining; and through it all ran Enrique's constant need for reassurance.

"Are you sure you're all right? Do you remember everything? Are you certain . . . ?"

"Yes, yes, and yes," I almost shouted. And then I added joyfully, "And you didn't go to La Cor . . . to Santander."

"No, I'd only gone a few miles when I began worrying about you, and decided to return. I've been afraid for you ever since Feli was found in your coat, but I kept telling myself that I was being melodramatic, that there was no reason for anyone to harm you . . ."

"But you came back."

"Yes, I felt wrong about leaving you, about everything. When I got back, Carlos met me in the hall and told me that you had been upset this afternoon, but that Paca had taken charge and you were now sleeping. I was just going off to check on you when your friend Meredith showed up."

"Edward?" I was so startled I almost jumped. "What was he doing here?"

"Storming the castle," Enrique answered drily. "Very politely but very determinedly. He explained that he'd been called back to the United States unexpectedly and permanently, but he'd found himself, while en route from Madrid, with rather a long layover in Bilbao and realizing that Bilbao wasn't all that far from 'us' (translated 'you'), he thought it would be a good time to look in on 'us' ('you'), and so had taken a plane to La Coruña, hired a car, and driven on here. He'd hoped to hear from 'us' ('you') again, and had left his forwarding address in Lugo, but he hadn't heard, and how were we anyway?"

"I suppose you insulted him?" I asked, my voice warming in spite of myself.

"No. I decided that Meredith, turning up in what he knew was hostile territory, when he was on his way home on urgent business, pressed for time but coming here anyway, had to be genuinely concerned for you. I guessed he'd gotten as far as Bilbao, started worrying about you and decided he couldn't leave Spain for good without checking on you again."

"So what did you do?" I asked, highly interested in this encounter.

"Invited him in for a drink, assured him I'd wake you to say good-bye before he left, and ended up by telling him something of your amnesia and how matters had stood since your coming home. Then he told me about your being shot at that day. That set my nerves jangling again, but I reminded myself that you were safe upstairs."

"Did he stay long?"

"No. He seemed reassured after we'd talked a bit, and when he started to leave he insisted that I not disturb you, gave me his card, and asked if we could be in touch. I said that we would be. We parted friends."

"It's hard to believe, but I'll take your word for it."

"And he'd barely gotten out the door before things really fell in on me. Grandmother returned without Nita, and I went tearing up the stairs and found you missing, Paca snoring blissfully. When I finally got her awake, she remembered the note . . ."

"And how were your nerves by then?" I asked, relishing every word.

"Banging like kettledrums. I started off for the River Cave in a dead run, and I run pretty well with orchestrated nerves. Paca rounded the others up and followed."

"You met Nita on the way?"

"Yes. She hadn't made it very far and she was frightened, but she told me what had happened, and insisted on going back to see if you were all right. Paca, who had shown up by then, took her home, under protest."

Darling Nita, refusing to be intimidated

by Father Fernando's threats. Thinking of her I stumbled again.

"Another rest stop," Enrique said, making me settle onto a large boulder. He had long ago taken off his raincoat and wrapped me in it, buckling me cozily in, with the belt tightened to half its size.

"Will you tell the villagers about Father Fernando and how he was at the last?" I asked.

"Do you wish me to?"

"No."

A wind sprang up, singing among the heather. Enrique stood in front of me, and at last he reached for my hand and took it in his, bending his fingers hard against my own.

"I agree. Father Fernando was revered and beloved in the village. There can be no purpose served now in revealing that he was mad, that he was a murderer. Alfredo and Pepe are bringing his body from the cave, and with the connivance of Dr. Martinez and Father Domingo, the word can be sent out that he died in his sleep, a heart attack. Then he can be buried with all the ceremonial reverence that he loved . . . but did not deserve."

"Never mind," I said contentedly.

Enclosed, safe now as I was, with

Enrique's fingers twined in mine, I found it difficult to believe what had happened to me in the last few hours.

And how could I not pity a dead man, when I was so shiningly alive? This aliveness was making me feel real again and curious about the machinations that had forced me to the cave.

"Can you guess how Father Fernando brought off the complicated timetable that made it certain I would follow Nita and him? When did he leave the note, I wonder? Why didn't someone see him?"

"Probably someone did. You forget that Father Fernando worked behind a cover of total trust on all sides. He could move about inside our house unquestioned, and he could maneuver in the village as he pleased. I think I can guess fairly accurately what occurred."

Undoubtedly (Enrique explained) the news of the plan for my leaving Galicia must have reached Father Fernando early in the afternoon. Fearful that my abrupt departure would put me out of his reach, he had driven as fast as possible to the Fuentes.

There he had gone to Nita's room, written the note, and left it. Knowing it was the señorita's half day, and knowing my habit of always seeking Nita out after the siesta hour, he had had no fear that I should miss the note, or not be the first to see it.

Then he had taken Anna, gone back to the village, and invited Nita to visit with him (something she did often) while Doña Carmen finished her calls.

It must have been during this time that he took his processional robes from the church, along with a sharp silver paper knife, which Alfredo found on his body.

According to Nita's story, Father Fernando took her to the cave, and ordered her to sit well inside. He then cut Anna to pieces with the paper knife. After that, his damaged brain requiring this of him, evidently, he had gone through the ritualistic donning of his robes and had hidden in the dark, near the cave entrance, to wait for me.

How he must have enjoyed this waiting, certain of me at last.

Remembering, I felt my fingers grow cold inside Enrique's, and he said abruptly, "Where shall we spend our honeymoon? Madrid?"

I surprised myself by answering, "Not Madrid."

I thought of my years of growing up there, wonderfully happy years with my improvident, young-hearted parents, whom I had adored. I remembered living in the Generalissimo area, just as Enrique had said. I remembered the apartment, spacious, filled with sunlight and flowers and beautiful half-paid-for furniture, and streams of friends as flighty and fascinating as my parents.

"Some day I want to go back. But not yet."

I didn't add that I needed time to get ready for that particular set of memories, but Enrique's radar was working overtime.

"Well, that's a relief. I thought you might say 'yes.' "

"You don't like Madrid?" I asked, totally diverted.

"Why should I like Madrid? Blaring taxi horns, six million people all talking at once, and all that boring sunlight. Besides I might run into Carlos."

"Carlos has gone to live in Madrid for good then?"

"Yes. Our first remittance man."

A sigh of relief escaped me. "How did you manage it?"

"Bought him off, subsidizing him from the running funds of the estate, using his share of the California property as security."

As delighted as I was at the news of Carlos' permanent departure, the mention of the California property disturbed me, and I said unhappily, "Does the offer from

California still stand?"

"I don't know. I've been too distracted by your illness and your leaving to even inquire. But if it's too late for this offer, there'll be others now. You are not to worry. Not about anything."

Enrique, always the one to comfort. I thought of how things had been for him since the accident, with me hating and fearing him, his every attempt to protect me resisted.

"Forgive me, Enrique."

He did not pretend to misunderstand, but pressed his fingers harder against mine. Silent forgiveness only, then. There must be other lingering wounds, like acid burns that wouldn't heal.

"It was only my daytime mind that distrusted you. You were always there in essence . . . the man I dreamed of, night after night."

"You often called out in your sleep, but you never called my name."

"I didn't recognize you until you walked away from me into the cave . . ."

Still, Enrique didn't speak, but a tautness I'd felt in him since the moment I'd opened my eyes in the hospital, seemed to melt from his body.

He swung around and caught me to him,

burying his face in my hair. Then, inevitably, his lips found mine and he laid a blazing kiss across my mouth.

When I could breathe again, I pulled away. I had an unhealed wound, myself, one that burned fierily when I thought back over the afternoon.

"Now what?" Enrique asked.

"Antonia."

"Antonia? What, I wonder, is there to say about Antonia?"

"I overheard you together the night I arrived. She sounded exactly like a demanding mistress," and then I added hotly, "your mistress."

"And what did I sound like?"

"Goaded. Placating."

"Exactly. All I could think of that night was getting my tiresome visitor out of the room as easily as I could, so I could start wondering what in the hell I was going to do about you and the maddening way you were carrying on."

"You could have told her to leave."

"No. There was a time, years ago, when Antonia and I had a bit of a fling, before she married my cousin. After he died, she could never get it through her head that I was no longer interested in starting in where we'd left off. But I had some rather strong feelings on the subject of rejection. I preferred not to state the case too clearly."

That stopped me for a minute, until I remembered something. "All very charitable," I replied, "but I happen to know you went to her room to see her, after you left me this afternoon. I heard you."

"Yes. To tell her to clear out and not return."

This was more like it. "Why?"

"Because I found that what you let drop about her and Alfredo, the night of the procession, was true. What Antonia does in Madrid or Barcelona is her business, but that sort of thing doesn't go down well around here. Such a scandal would have reached my grandmother eventually and disturbed her very much."

"Well, why was Antonia practically allowed to move in, in the first place? Talk about a star boarder, she was it!"

"I don't know what a 'star boarder' is, but as the wife of my dead cousin, I could not deny her the hospitality of my house. Not until she abused that hospitality."

"Very Spanish," I answered. And very satisfying. But I couldn't resist adding, "It's just as well things have worked out this way, because I've seen all I want to see of Antonia. I didn't care for her devious ways.

For one thing, she had that dreadful old woman above the bakery spying on me. Very nerve-racking."

"You must mean old Margarita. Ancient and harmless, a retainer from Antonia's family, who had no place to go, no relatives. When Antonia and my cousin married, they brought her here to the village, set her up, gave her a small pension, and forgot her."

"Not entirely. Her place made an excellent base of operations, when Antonia was Lisa watching."

"Why was Antonia watching you?"

"I was never quite sure. Trying to keep track of Edward and me, I suppose. Hoping I'd run off with him, get off the scene . . ."

"Well, it's no longer important, is it? The important thing is that I must write to your San Francisco doctors, telling them of your recovery. At their request, I've corresponded with them, and kept a diary of your situation. I recorded the diary in Spanish, because it was quicker and easier for me. But it must be translated before we send it."

"I'll help," I replied in a rush, newly alarmed.

Enrique must never know that I had read the "Lisa" folder, nor must he know of my suspicions afterward. These suspicions would be the one thing he could never forgive. They could inflict the one wound that would not heal. But my alarm subsided when I realized that he was sidetracked on another grievance.

"You never wore your aquamarine pin but once."

"I thought you bought it for Antonia."

"Lisa, you are the most exasperating creature! What made you think that?"

"Because I decided that if it had been for me, you would have bought it before the crash . . ."

"I did buy it before the crash. I was going to give you the pin on our wedding night. I carried it all that day in my pocket, and somehow it got through the smash-up. When I took it out and looked at it later, there wasn't a scratch on it."

So the aquamarine, like me, had survived, whole, unscathed, safe in Enrique's care. Because I felt a ridiculous inclination to cry, I got to my feet, saying lightly, "Well, I must get home and unpack."

As we started out again, Enrique, drawing my arm through his, made a suggestion. "While you're there, you might try washing your face. I'm tired of kissing that mud-pack you're wearing."

My free hand flew to my cheek. I'd forgotten how awful I must look. "Am I very repellant?" I asked.

"Very," he answered, leaning down to kiss me again.